COMING ACROSS JORDAN

The Also Rans Series ②

COMING ACROSS JORDAN

Mabel Elizabeth Singletary

MOODY PUBLISHERS
CHICAGO

All Scripture quotations are taken from the King James Version.

Editor: Kathryn Hall
Interior Design: Ragont Design
Cover Design and Photography: TS Design Studio

Library of Congress Cataloging-in-Publication Data

Singletary, Mabel Elizabeth.
    Coming across Jordan / Mabel Elizabeth Singletary.
        p. cm. — (The Also Rans series ; bk. 2)
    Summary: Philadelphia sixth-graders Kevin and Melanie become fast friends as they encourage Jordan, an autistic kindergartener, to draw, but when they decide to paint a mural on school property they learn that even when they are doing good, there are boundaries.
    ISBN 978-0-8024-2259-0
    [1. Autism—Fiction. 2. Artists—Fiction. 3. Mural painting and decoration—Fiction. 4. Interpersonal relations—Fiction. 5. African Americans—Fiction. 6. Christian life—Fiction.] I. Title.

PZ7.S61767Com 2009
[Fic]—dc22

                                                        2008048600

1 3 5 7 9 10 8 6 4 2

Printed in the United States of America

For those who know that miracles seen,
begin in hearts that dare to believe.

CONTENTS

NEW KIDS

ON THE MORNING of January 19, a little more than a year ago, Harriet Tubman Elementary School in the city of Philadelphia welcomed a couple of new members to its student body. Usually, the arrival of new students to the building summoned the attention of every child from every grade, but somehow twelve-year-old Kevin Manning had managed to slip into the cafeteria virtually unnoticed. Small for his age, yet strikingly handsome, Kevin's shyness overshadowed his child-star good looks.

Most of his time was devoted to thinking about the one activity he really loved to do. Kevin Manning loved to draw. And he was the first to admit, if he had one wish, it would be that every class of the day could be art class. He placed his book bag beneath his seat and quietly sat down to eat his cereal.

Removing the lid from his cereal bowl, he thought about what it means to be "new." *How interesting*, he thought, *in any other situation, the word new means something wonderful, something current and unique.* Then he took the word new and paired it with as many things as his mind would allow. He thought of things like a new house, a new bike, and of course, new clothes and new sneakers.

No, Kevin couldn't put the word "new" in front of anything that meant something unpleasant—except when it was paired with "kid." He knew all too well that being a "new kid" in school brought its own set of challenges. Kevin had lived through the experience before, so one would have thought he could just accept getting past the "fitting in period" and wait it out until he had a chance to make some friends. Unfortunately, every time he began to feel cautiously comfortable, like when he'd stick his feet in the icy cold water at the beach, it was time to move on.

Since everyone's attention and most of the conversation centered on the lack of heat in the cold cafeteria, no one even noticed Kevin. And aside from being pleased about his obscure entrance, this was a memorable morning for a number of other reasons.

First, the frigid cold felt by staff and students alike was even more extreme than it had been the day before when everyone was declaring *that day* as having been the coldest. For the second time in three days, Mr. Turner, the school's custodian, was having a harder time than usual getting the boiler to work. His regular routine of kicking it, banging on it, and yelling at it, on this particular day produced no results. Secondly, at nineteen degrees, not only was it the coldest day of the year outside, it could officially go on record as the coldest day inside the walls of Harriet Tubman as well.

Mrs. Blake, one of the kindergarten teachers, advised her students, who were having breakfast, to sit quietly while eating. At the same time she cautioned them to keep their coats on. Like very young children are known to do, they followed their teacher's direction to the letter. The boys and girls who made up her homeroom sat bundled up like little Eskimos in their coats, hats, and scarves. Some were quietly eating spoonfuls of hot cereal, while others dipped rectangular pieces of graham crackers deeply into their cartons of icy white milk.

Many of the older students sat with fingers crossed, hoping to hear an announcement at any moment from Mr. Tate, the principal, declaring that school was cancelled and everyone would be going home for the day. However, one sixth-grader named Melanie Clark wisely believed that—short of the bricks that made up the building being dismantled and the walls coming apart at its seams—there was no chance of anyone going home.

Melanie had a reputation for being talkative, but was equally recognized for her independent sense of style and overall uniqueness. She prided herself on what she considered her ability to "come across things." She liked to credit herself with making all kinds of discoveries. And whether these discoveries centered around new recipes, other countries, or interesting people, she liked to think that sharing what she learned had a positive effect on others.

Upon meeting her, the first thing you'd notice was her hair. She wore it up in a natural style and bound it all together by tying a colorful bandana around it. She was proud to boast that the bandanas she wore were made from genuine Kente cloth that her mother had brought back for her from a trip to Nigeria. And Melanie always wore each one of them proudly. She also owned a jacket, a skirt, and a matching belt made of Kente as well.

Melanie loved reading about the countries that made up the continent of Africa and bragged that one day when she was "all grown up," she'd go there and see them for herself. For now, though, she had to settle for gazing at the globe that sat on top of the desk in her bedroom. She'd spin it and watch it whirl around and around. Just before it stopped, she'd take her index finger and let it land on one of the far away countries that make up the world she longed to see someday.

Melanie was also very proud of her status as a sixth-grader and considered herself to be somewhat of a "goodwill ambassador" at Harriet Tubman. When it came to welcoming new students, she stepped right up to the plate and greeted them with a great big "hello." She especially enjoyed watching the younger kids as they sat together and made every effort to closely follow the rules and do whatever their teachers told them. And it wasn't out of the ordinary for her to share her observations with her friends and tell them how naïve she thought the little six-year-olds were.

"So young and so innocent," she'd sigh. "Those little guys haven't been in school long enough to even know they've got choices. But things'll be normal by the time they get to third grade . . . I hope."

Everyone sitting at the sixth-grade table laughed at Melanie's belief about why the little kids were so obedient. Thinking about what she'd said even caused her to laugh again. But in a moment, as though the sixth-graders sitting with her were part of some great orchestra following the baton of a famous conductor, everything stopped—including the laughter.

All the attention moved to the sight of a young boy being led toward the table where Mrs. Blake's students sat quietly finishing the rest of their breakfast. And this was the third reason why this particular day stood apart from most.

"Mrs. Blake," the school secretary called with a slight melody in her voice, "this is Jordan Manning. He's six years old and he'll be joining your kindergarten class today." In spite of the upbeat way she spoke, one only had to look a little closer to see her shake her head when she handed Mrs. Blake a plain manila folder. When she turned to leave the cafeteria, her steps no longer matched the pleasantness heard in her voice only moments ago.

It was interesting to watch how she had physically directed the little boy to a spot where his new teacher waited for him. It was as if, without her leading, he wouldn't have moved an inch on his own. Just as intriguing to watch were the other children in Mrs. Blake's class as they continued to eat as though nothing out of the ordinary had happened.

Only a few seconds went by before Mrs. Brundidge, an older rotund woman, who was head of the entire cafeteria staff, stepped out from the kitchen to see what was going on. When she realized she was about to add another name to the list of students who came for breakfast, she smiled.

Mrs. Brundidge spoke with a heavy German accent. She loved children, and the children at Harriet Tubman loved her too. The more she fed them, the better it made her feel. She had her own theory about how to keep children happy. She believed the way to make happy children is to make sure they have good food to eat—especially in the morning.

"An who'd dis might be?" she asked as she put her hands on her hips, clearly displaying the fact that she was in charge. Then she wiped both hands on her apron and placed one hand gently on Jordan's shoulder.

"Oon, yes, I dink you would like some good cereal to eat. Yes?" When the young boy didn't answer her, she looked to Mrs. Blake for an explanation.

"This is Jordan," she said, smiling. "This is his first day. And you're right, Mrs. Brundidge, I'm sure he would like some cereal."

Hearing Mrs. Blake agree with her made Mrs. Brundidge light up all over. She quickly hustled back to the kitchen. Even though breakfast time was pretty much over, she returned with a small bowl of cereal, a carton of milk, and a plastic spoon just for Jordan. "Dis good for you," she told him. "You will grow and be de strongest of dem all."

Mrs. Blake took it upon herself to accept Mrs. Brundidge's good wishes for her newest student. "Thank you, Mrs. Brundidge."

"Danke," she said softly and headed back into the kitchen.

Then Mrs. Blake called to a little boy with flaming red hair and lots of freckles. "Danny, please raise your hand." She pointed to a seat next to the little boy who had raised his hand. "You can sit there," she told Jordan.

Danny only looked away from his cereal for a moment. He did, however, take a couple of seconds to flash a great big smile at his new classmate. Then, in the blink of an eye, he used the sleeve of his coat to wipe away some milk that had dripped from his mouth, picked up his bowl, and quickly gulped down the rest. Jordan, however, didn't move and he didn't smile back. He just stood there as though confused about what he was supposed to do.

Mrs. Blake was still holding the cereal, milk, and spoon Mrs. Brundidge had given her for Jordan. And she knew if he didn't have something to eat soon, he would probably be hungry for most of the morning, since it was almost time for class to start. Known for being one of the nicest teachers at Tubman, she easily could have won an award for being one of the most patient ones too.

That was certainly one of the major reasons why Melanie considered Mrs. Blake to be her favorite teacher of all time. If there was anything she could do to help her students learn, she did it. And as hard as she tried, Melanie couldn't remember Mrs. Blake ever coming into class without a smile on her face. Somehow her sweet and caring disposition made everyone around her feel special.

So it was easy to see why, in Melanie's opinion, she was unquestionably the best teacher in the whole world. Any time Mrs. Blake's name came up in a conversation, Melanie could be heard telling those around her that of all the teachers she'd had in her seven years of schooling, none of them even came close to being as nice as Mrs. Blake. And as far as Melanie Clark was concerned, the new kid named Jordan was lucky to get the chance to be in her class. Watching carefully, she listened as Mrs. Blake introduced herself to her newest student.

And just as Melanie predicted, Mrs. Blake bent down, like she was known to do, and gave herself the opportunity to communicate with little Jordan at eye level. She reached out to shake his hand. However, one didn't have to look real close to sense the sadness she felt when he failed to lift either of his hands to return the gesture. Instead, Jordan stood silently like a rigid little soldier with both hands at his sides, waiting for someone to give a command.

His eyes stared straight ahead, seeing, yet not seeing, the things right in front of him. Jordan was a handsome little boy with caramel-colored skin and rich, dark brown eyes that looked like circles of delicious chocolate. Eyes that you could get lost in, because no matter how hard or how deeply you searched, they always led to the same place—nowhere.

In what little time she had, Mrs. Blake's eyes studied her newest pupil for even the smallest outward sign of happiness. If she had to name one single thing that had watered her desire many years ago to teach kindergarten, it was the joy and laughter that seemed to go hand in hand with being a six-year-old. Unfortunately, not even the slightest inkling of joy could be detected in Jordan. Her eyes examined the young boy again; only this time more carefully. As if by instinct, she opened the folder and found her suspicions to be true. There staring her in the face was the word that defined Jordan's unusual behavior. And though reluctant to say it out loud, she faintly whispered that word to herself: *Autism.*

"Look at that little kid," Melanie said, steering even more of the attention of those at the table toward the new boy. And to make sure no one missed her announcement, she pointed as well. "That's gotta be the first little kid I ever saw who looked like he didn't wanna be here. I won't be getting in his way. No sir, I wouldn't wanna have to tangle with him 'cause I think I'd lose in a minute."

A boy sitting next to her agreed. "Yeah, he sure don't look too happy 'bout being in school. And he's not even old enough yet to know he ain't supposed to be happy. Look at all the rest of them other little kids! They don't have a clue they ain't supposed to be so glad about bein' here."

At the far end of the table next to Melanie's, Kevin sat quietly eating his breakfast. He was content that he was able to do so in peace. While a part of him felt sad for the younger boy because by now every eye in the cafeteria was on him, another part of him was happy that none of that curious carnival-kind of attention had traveled in his direction.

No one, he thought, *wants to be so new or so different that everybody's staring at you like you're standing in the middle of a bull's eye. And worst than that*, his thoughts continued, *is when everyone is staring at you and you don't seem to know they're staring.* Kevin watched the other students gawking at Jordan as though he had just landed on earth from another planet. On the outside, he allowed himself to feel some guilt, but on the inside, he was relieved that he wasn't the object of so much attention.

Kevin gave himself permission to lower his eyes and continued eating his cereal in silence. Like Melanie, he was a sixth-grader too. But unlike the others at her table, twelve-year-old Kevin didn't think the comments they made were the least bit funny. He did find it both strange and confusing that Melanie would be the first one to point out the new boy's differences, when she looked nothing like any of the other kids sitting around her.

Surely, with being fully dressed from head to toe in African garb, she didn't look like anyone Kevin had ever seen before. Hoping no one saw him, he tried to inch himself slightly away from the kids sitting near him and get closer to the wall all the way at the end where the table stopped.

"Look," said the boy sitting next to Melanie. "That kid won't even sit down!"

Kevin could feel his muscles tensing up and his heartbeat began racing. He prayed that his body language wouldn't reveal just how annoyed he was starting to feel. He'd been in the building no more than thirty minutes and was already becoming extremely uncomfortable. Like any twelve-year-old, Kevin wanted to be liked and accepted by the other kids at his new school. After all, this was an expectation and a right that he believed every sixth-grader was entitled to.

He was absolutely sure if he conducted a poll and asked every sixth-grader in the cafeteria, they'd all agree that they deserved a special place among their peers just because they occupied the highest grade level in the school. And one could easily tell by the way most of them walked, they felt empowered because their peers shared the same opinions about the world around them and everything in it.

Yet, as much as Kevin yearned to be a part of this new group, he was fully aware of an even greater sense of loyalty to someone who meant more to him than attaining a special place on the social hierarchy. Still, most of the time the feeling he harbored in his heart could be exhausting, but he nonetheless acknowledged his responsibility. Having been born first in a family of two children set him on a course that at times caused him to wish he was invisible.

Through no choice of his own, in addition to inheriting the title "big brother," he likewise acquired the title of "protector." All he had to do was close his eyes and he could hear his mother admonishing him, "take care of your brother, he needs you."

Kevin sometimes wondered if those around him realized that he needed someone to look after him too. For now, he was just glad he wouldn't have to assert himself in any way. He didn't want to let anyone in the cafeteria know he usually had to be "more" than most twelve-year-olds were expected to be. Kevin Manning was often expected to be brave in the face of criticism and ready to aid his younger brother at a moment's notice.

From his secure place at the end of the table, he watched Jordan as he stood motionless in front of his new teacher and class-mates. *"Smile,"* Kevin mouthed silently. With everything inside of him, in a hushed voice, he urged the younger boy to try. One would have thought he was cheering on a friend who was on the verge of making the winning touchdown in the big game. *"Please,"* he pleaded. *"For once . . . just smile,"* Kevin urged.

Suddenly, Kevin's face mirrored the same sadness he'd seen in Mrs. Blake's eyes just seconds ago. But his expression had an-other feature as well—panic. He could feel something was about to happen and with everything inside of him, he prayed that maybe this time things would be different. *After all*, he encour-aged himself, *it's a new day, and we're in a new school.* However, right on the tail end of his thought, Kevin could feel a familiar scene about to rewind and getting ready to play itself for all the world to see.

Before he even had the chance to finish eating his cereal, he heard it. That blood-curdling scream that could blow the roof off of any school building filled the room. The little boy with his hands at his sides, who appeared to stare off into nowhere, was screaming at the top of his lungs. And no one had even the faintest idea about what to do to stop it. Many of the children in Mrs. Blake's class cupped their tiny hands over their ears and rocked their heads back and forth while yelling "stop!"

Kevin wanted to cry because he knew his brief period of peace had, at that very moment, come to an end. He was no stranger to the word Mrs. Blake had seen in the manila folder. Six-year-old Jordan Manning was autistic *and he was Kevin's little brother.* He knew he couldn't remain anonymous any longer. So he got up from his seat and sauntered over to Jordan. Speaking in his softest voice and reaching for the bowl of cereal, he spoke to Mrs. Blake.

"May I have it?" he asked, putting out his hand. Without asking why, she handed it to him. And the second she gave it to him, the new boy named Kevin gently placed the bowl into Jordan's small hands. "It's okay, Jordan," he said. "It's okay."

Just as unexpected as the onset of the strange screaming had begun, in a breath, it was just as abruptly gone.

"Thank you," Mrs. Blake said as she helped Jordan sit down next to Danny.

Kevin, who had already started walking back to his seat, turned slightly and said almost in a whisper, "you're welcome." He immediately resolved that getting even a glimpse of the smile he'd hoped for wouldn't be coming out of Jordan on this very cold January morning. And as far as Kevin was concerned, the ringing of the first bell of the day couldn't have come at a better time. All the talk about Jordan stopped as the students got up and went to their homeroom classes. He was overly grateful that no one would have time to ask him any questions.

Melanie and the rest of the students at her table hustled to empty their trays and gather their things. Kevin felt relieved knowing, at least for now, the comments and questions about the unusual kindergarten student were over. He knew those were questions he didn't want to answer, and he also knew that his reprieve was only temporary. For as certain as he was about sharing the last name Manning with the little boy who had drawn so much attention, he knew his time was up. He would have to reprise his role as the "lone protector" of Jordan. And whether he wanted the job or not—it had chosen him—and not the other way around.

One of the trash bins was only steps away from the table where Mrs. Blake's class sat. So it was no surprise that it was the very one Melanie chose to dispose of her garbage. "Hi, Mrs. Blake!" she called as she slowed down to toss her milk container and cereal dish into the trash can. Since she had passed by two other garbage containers, it was plain to see that she had an ulterior motive for walking over to the area where the kindergarten students sat.

Melanie fixed her eyes on the new boy, allowing herself to get a real good look at him. At first glance, he appeared no different from the other children in Mrs. Blake's class. But no matter how many times Melanie walked near him, it was as if she wasn't there at all. She even tried to get his attention by waving her hand and saying hello.

The same children, who up to a moment ago had been so quiet, were now restless and moving around. They were making the usual kinds of noises that tend to accompany six-year-olds wherever they go. And as good as Mrs. Blake was at keeping her class quiet and orderly most of the time, even she wasn't infallible when it came to keeping twenty-two rambunctious kindergarten students intact every minute of the day.

As she lined up her students, she began to come face-to-face with the grim reality that Jordan was going to need more time than she knew she had to spare. "Somehow," she whispered, "with God's help, I've got to try and do what I can." That first bit of trying came the moment Mrs. Blake noticed Jordan had finished eating. She gently took her new student by the hand, hoping that somehow he would feel welcome. She led him, along with the rest of her group, out the door and down the corridor that led to her classroom.

Melanie and Kevin watched like careful guardians whose eyes followed the small train of children until the very last one had left the cafeteria. Kevin didn't have to wonder if Jordan would look back. He knew that he wouldn't.

"C'mon," Melanie summoned after noticing Kevin at the far end of the table. "I'll help ya find your class." Kevin smiled shyly and accepted her invitation. "Okay," he said. Relieved that he wouldn't have to find his way to his class alone, he got up from his seat. After disposing of his trash, he joined Melanie and the two of them walked toward the sixth-grade hallway. He was even more relieved that Melanie didn't ask him a hundred questions about what had just happened.

"That was pretty good the way you helped that new boy stop screaming. I don't think nobody else even knew what to do."

Kevin dropped his head. "Wasn't nothing special."

"I bet everybody in the cafeteria thought it was. Soon as you held his hands, he stopped. How'd you know to do that?"

Kevin paused as though wondering whether he should tell Melanie his secret.

"Guess I kinda knew what to do . . . 'cause Jordan is my little brother."

"That kid's your brother?" she sounded with surprise in her voice.

Kevin felt the discomfort coming back. "That a problem?"

"No, I just never saw that happen before."

"You mean the screaming like that?" he asked, letting down his guard a little.

"No." Melanie seemed more preoccupied with patting herself on the back about something else she had cleverly figured out. "I *knew* it," she announced. "I *knew* you were a new kid," she said, grinning ear to ear. She had made another one of her discoveries. "I could just tell," she said with all the confidence of a famous private eye who had just single handedly solved a great mystery. She looked at Kevin and declared, "You just didn't want nobody to know."

"Yeah," he responded politely, "I'm a new kid too."

Kevin gave way with half a smile at Melanie's comment. She was right in figuring out that he didn't want anyone to know. But the "cat was out of the bag" and all he could do now was step forward and hope there was a place for him to fit in at Harriet Tubman Elementary School in the great city of Philadelphia. *At least*, he thought, *walking to class with Melanie will cut down on the staring.* She had been there a while and maybe the other students would think he'd been there all along too. Kevin felt grateful for the possibility.

"Wow!" Melanie exclaimed, "I never came across two new kids in one day!"

Chapter 2

BEST TEACHER IN THE WORLD!

WEARING THE TITLE "sixth-grader" at Harriet Tubman brought along with it some built-in respectability. It really was a special place on the elementary school hierarchy where all the younger kids in the building wanted to be. If you were in the sixth grade, it meant you were only a breath away from entering middle school. And everyone knew entering middle school signaled the beginning of a whole new chapter in one's school life.

Still, as coveted a grade level as it may have been, no grade could ever compete with the kind of magnetic pull Melanie had for Mrs. Blake's kindergarten classroom. From time to time she still thought about how good it felt almost seven years ago when each morning as she stepped into the classroom, Mrs. Blake greeted every one of her students with a warm smile. So finding Melanie waiting at her door at least three times each week after dismissal was nothing unusual.

Melanie always made sure when she arrived before the children had gone for the day, if there was anything she could do to help them, she did so right away. She enjoyed working with the younger children and felt good knowing how much they looked up to her. But it wasn't all one-sided either. Melanie knew that she gained as much from the admiration they felt for her as they did every time one of them screamed and squealed with joy because she'd helped them place that last puzzle piece successfully into its flat wooden picture cutout.

As odd as it may have seemed to some, at the ripe old age of twelve, Melanie had made up her mind to become a teacher someday. She was quick to tell her friends it was an easy decision after the wonderful year she'd spent as a kindergarten student in Mrs. Blake's class.

So Melanie's plan to show up on this day was no exception from a practice she had begun long ago. She sat at her desk crossing her legs back and forth while waiting for that last bell of the day to ring. And although he had a different reason for wanting to hear the bell, Kevin was just as anxious as Melanie for it to sound. It would mean that his first day at Tubman was done. Once he made sure Jordan was safely home, he could spend some time drawing and lose himself in his art.

When Kevin began to draw, it was as if no one else was around. He would sketch peaceful pictures of orange-colored sunsets and beautiful birds playfully crisscrossing and soaring above the horizon. It was a time of day for him that never came fast enough. And though he never complained about watching his little brother, as they were both growing, it was certainly becoming a lot harder for him.

Maybe part of the problem for Kevin was the routine. Every day until his mom got home from work, he had the job of being responsible for Jordan. Usually, he'd give him his little toy truck. And as long as Jordan could repeatedly turn its tiny black wheels, he would stay right beside Kevin. Knowing Jordan wouldn't move gave Kevin permission to freely draw colorful pictures of the things he liked.

When he was especially proud of something he'd drawn, he would point and say, "Look, Jordan! That's a bird," or "That's an oak tree." And even though he got no response, there was something about the innocent look in his little brother's eyes that showed the amazement one sees when something beautiful has been discovered for the first time. Maybe that was the reason Kevin often wished he could take his little brother by the hand and the two of them could become part of the scenes he drew, while pretending they led to some great unknown adventure.

He glanced over at Jordan still turning the wheels, and the spell was broken. They would probably never know what it was like to be two brothers running, jumping, climbing, and chasing adventure. Kevin understood that he would have to settle for gazing into his own drawings and using his imagination in order to have the kind of fun his heart told him brothers were supposed to have.

Kevin sensed that Jordan liked his drawings, so the walls of the room they shared were covered with them. In a way, their tiny bedroom offered the same serenity one could find in Mrs. Blake's classroom. It was small, yet comfortable and attractive.

Knowing the end of the day countdown was only seconds away caused Kevin to start counting backward in his head. *Ten, nine, eight, seven, six, five, four, three, two, one* . . . *yes!* He shouted in his brain and pretended to spring out of his seat. As far as he was concerned, after hearing his homeroom teacher say the word "dismissed," he was now free to be the one thing he wanted to be more than anything else in the world. Kevin Manning wanted to be an artist.

Melanie was surprised when she noticed the new boy staring at the clock. And she was even more surprised that he successfully managed to bolt out of the room before she did. It rarely happened that Melanie wasn't the first student out of the room at dismissal time. She hurried out the door to catch up with Kevin.

"Wanna go to Mrs. Blake's room with me? She's got fish and all kinds of other good stuff!"

Kevin's mind was on one thing and that was getting his brother and going home. Melanie frowned when it appeared that he was taking too long to give her an answer. *After all,* she thought, *how could anyone pass up a chance to see Mrs. Blake's tank of tropical fish?* It just didn't make sense to her that Kevin wouldn't jump at the invitation.

She soon understood that Kevin hadn't fully heard all of what she'd said. But once he zeroed in on the words, "and all kinds of other good stuff," he turned around. And with his eyes widened real big, he asked, "what'd you say? . . . something 'bout good stuff? . . . like what?"

Melanie looked at him with all the satisfaction of the Cheshire cat from Alice in Wonderland. She had baited the hook and was sure Kevin was being reeled in by her invitation. The words "other good stuff" had whet his palate of curiosity. And

Melanie was determined to keep pulling him in until he conceded that he would accompany her to Mrs. Blake's room.

The last thing Kevin wanted to do was start off on the wrong foot at his new school. One way he thought that could happen might be by hanging around a girl—especially a girl who seemed to talk a whole lot like Melanie does. However, putting her talking aside, the more he thought about it, the more he found himself drawn to those irresistible words "and other good stuff." He just couldn't resist. His mind was made up. So he hoisted his book bag over his shoulder and followed his new friend down the corridor straight to Mrs. Blake's room.

When they got there, they peeked inside but didn't go in. Kevin could see Jordan sitting in a chair in the back of the room where Mrs. Blake was talking to him and tying his shoelaces. Surely it wasn't an easy task for her. Kevin had tied his brother's shoes many times before and knew it took great skill and creativity to get the right results. He watched attentively from the doorway. Every time Mrs. Blake tried to make a loop with one of the shoestrings, Jordan's right foot would swing continuously.

Kevin was surprised that Mrs. Blake seemed to understand and accepted the fact that he couldn't help it. So instead of telling him to stop, she moved her hands along with the swing of his foot and when the two were in sync, she was somehow able to successfully tie his shoe without having him stop moving. "See what I mean?" Melanie said pointing. "Mrs. Blake is amazing."

The rest of the children were already gone for the day. Melanie and Kevin had passed Mrs. Duncan, one of the school aides, in the hallway. She was walking a group of children to their waiting buses, while Mrs. Blake stayed behind with her new student. She had been informed that Jordan was to wait for his older brother to pick him up. "I'm glad I'm a walker," Melanie said proudly. "That means we can stay as long as we want. Plus, Mrs. Blake's the best teacher in the whole world!"

"I'll wait here," Kevin insisted. He knew he needed to go inside to get his little brother, but still chose to stay in the hallway. He just wasn't ready. Crossing the threshold of the classroom meant he was once again responsible for Jordan.

"Fine with me," Melanie said, pretending not to care. "You're the one who's gonna miss out." Without looking back at her new friend, she smiled the biggest smile she knew how and went inside the classroom. Melanie immediately went over to where Mrs. Blake was talking to Jordan and joined them. And while her intention was to speak to Mrs. Blake, her real focus was planted squarely on the quiet little boy she found to be so interesting.

"Hi, Mrs. Blake," she said as though making an announcement. "Anything I can do to help ya today?"

Mrs. Blake's eyes searched around the room, hoping to find a task for Melanie to do. She looked back at the door where she could see Kevin waiting outside. "Doesn't your friend want to come in?"

By now, Kevin had begun pacing in the hallway. He knew he had to go inside. It was time to take Jordan home. Plus, there was that secret part of him that really wanted to get a look at those tropical fish. He was sure if he looked in a mirror, he'd see the word "interested" written all over him. If the truth were known, that's what all the moving around was about. Kevin thought if he kept moving, his desire to join Melanie and Jordan wouldn't be as strong.

"That's Jordan's brother, Kevin . . . he said he wasn't comin' in."

"I remember him from this morning. We've been waiting for him, haven't we, Jordan?" Mrs. Blake stood up. "I'll tell him to come in."

Melanie wondered if getting a personal invitation from Mrs. Blake might help Kevin change his mind about joining them. She could see Mrs. Blake saying something but wasn't able to hear what she was saying. She did, however, see Kevin nodding his head yes and then quietly walk in behind her. She wasn't at all surprised. Somehow, Mrs. Blake always found the right words to say to make the students at Harriet Tubman feel good.

Melanie immediately ran up to Kevin and summoned him to join her and Jordan in the back of the classroom. Kevin responded by waving his hand no and remained about eight steps away from the door. She, in turn, questioned his decision with her eyes and returned to the area of the room where she felt at ease and comfortable.

"He said no," she told Jordan.

Reaching for a box of colored wooden blocks, she began stacking them in front of him. "Here," she said. "This is red." Melanie gently took Jordan's hands and placed the red block into them. "Red," she said again, "red block." She helped him put the block on the table and took another one. "Blue," she told him. "This one's blue. Go ahead, say blue."

Mrs. Blake saw Melanie trying to guide Jordan and knew how much she loved helping out, but could also see her becoming a little frustrated. She quietly reminded Melanie that it was Jordan's first day and by having the right amount of patience, she could one day expect wonderful results. Her words were calm and supportive and they allowed Melanie to stop pushing so hard.

"Here, Jordan," she said, handing him a bright green block. "You can play with this one."

Mrs. Blake folded her arms and lightly tapped her foot. She figured Melanie might be ready to try something else. "Hmm . . . let me see. I would appreciate it if you'd neatly stack those papers on that table in the corner. Maybe you can put them in alphabetical order. What do you think?"

Melanie's eyes sparkled like Christmas ornaments. But when she took a good look at how many papers there were, she thought maybe she'd spoken a little too soon.

"Sure," she said. The great big smile that had adorned her face only a few seconds ago had pretty much disappeared. Getting up, she made her way to a large round table in the back corner of the room and sat down. Holding up a paper and waving it, she smiled at Jordan warmly and made him an offer.

"Wanna help?" Getting no response from him didn't seem to bother her one bit. She was already starting to practice the patience Mrs. Blake had told her about. Instead of getting annoyed, she started separating the pile of papers by first finding all the ones having last names beginning with A, and then moved on to last names beginning with the letter B.

Whenever Melanie visited Mrs. Blake's room, it was as if she had entered for the first time. She always made it a point to look around the whole room. If anything new had been added, like a poster or a new bulletin board, she was sure to notice it. And the one thing Melanie loved the most about Mrs. Blake's classroom was the color. Nothing compared with the warmth that the burst of bright colors seemed to bring. From the moment one entered—from the ceiling to the floor—everything breathed rich, radiant, glowing color. All of the charts, pictures, letters, and numbers came alive with the vibrant greens, blues, and yellows adorning each and every wall of the room.

As she sat and arranged the papers, Melanie thought about how good she felt all over on the days when she stopped by. In fact, just anticipating the afternoons when she planned to visit made her work harder in class because she knew when she arrived, Mrs. Blake would ask about her studies. Knowing her former teacher would shower her with big congratulations, she readily shared news about good papers and test grades. Melanie knew from the moment she stepped over the threshold that separated this classroom from all the others that lined either side of the hallway—good things were sure to happen.

Once all the papers were in alphabetical order, it took no time at all for Melanie to neatly arrange them into a nice pile. And pretty soon, she was standing right in front of Mrs. Blake, waiting for something else to do. As patient as Melanie tried to be, she knew what she wanted to do next. Not able to wait another second, she blurted out her request. With excitement in her eyes, she pleaded, "May I feed the fish?"

Mrs. Blake glanced over at Jordan who was sitting quietly in a chair. The red and blue blocks remained on the table in front of him while he still held the green one in his hands.

"Maybe Jordan would like to feed the fish with you," Mrs. Blake suggested. "And maybe his brother would like to help too."

"You mean Kevin?" Melanie seemed surprised. "He's just standin' there."

Mrs. Blake wasn't one to give up easily. "Maybe we can try one more time to get him to change his mind."

"Okay," Melanie conceded. "I'll try." It was a very short walk from the back of the room to where Kevin had positioned himself in the front. Melanie wasn't sure what she was supposed to say but was willing to make another attempt to see if she could get Kevin to join them. This time she boldly stepped up to him and stared him in the eyes. "You scared?"

"I ain't scared of nothin'," Kevin responded fearlessly.

"Then come back and help us feed the fish. They can't bite."

Kevin was annoyed. "I told you, I ain't scared." Before Melanie could say anything else, Kevin started walking toward the huge fish tank. But when he got to the back of the room, he still kept his distance. For right now Melanie found herself more curious about Jordan and how he'd like the fish rather than caring about what Kevin thought. She remembered how she had seen Mrs. Blake gently take him by the hand so she did the same.

"C'mon," she said, leading him slowly toward the fish tank. "Let's feed the fish." Melanie sensed easiness in the way he held her hand and knew right away, it was all right with him. Without saying a word, Jordan allowed her to guide him to the huge rectangular fish tank. Just like the rest of the room, it was also alive with a sea of color. Without moving his body, Jordan stood in front of the tank. He allowed his eyes to follow the fish as they swam from one end to the other, competing for the pellets of fish food that Melanie shook into the top of the tank.

While Melanie fed the fish and Jordan watched, Mrs. Blake

believed it was the right time to get Kevin involved. "Would you like to try?" she asked.

"Naw, I'm okay." The way Kevin stretched his neck to see what Melanie was doing gave the impression he wanted to feed the fish too. Mrs. Blake noticed Kevin looking at the fun Melanie was having and decided to give it yet another try. "Sure you don't want to feed the fish? I just added some new gold ones the other day."

As much as he wanted to be strong enough to resist the offer, Kevin's curiosity got the better of him. First, he moved a little closer to the tank. Within seconds he found himself standing right next to Melanie and Jordan. If anyone had asked him, he wouldn't have been able to tell exactly how the move had happened. However, the second he allowed himself to admit he thought the fish tank was fascinating, his two feet took charge and moved him as close as he could get.

While standing there gazing into the beautiful, rich blue water, Kevin began to understand why Melanie was so excited about coming to Mrs. Blake's room. Even the softness of the carpet under his feet felt good and inviting as he quietly stepped across the room.

When Melanie finished feeding the fish, she pressed her face against the glass tank and proceeded to open and close her mouth as though pretending she was a fish too. She hoped doing that would make Jordan laugh. "Look at me!" she told Jordan. "Look at me! Watch me do what they're doing!" She remembered when she had done this before with some of the children in Mrs. Blake's class, how they laughed and tried to imitate her behavior. Then, they'd all laugh together. But Jordan didn't laugh.

She moved her face away from the glass, backed up, and

stared into his deep brown eyes. "What's wrong?" she asked him. "You don't like the fish? All little kids like fish, don't they, Mrs. Blake?"

Mrs. Blake didn't answer because she was watching Kevin, who, though silent, now seemed to want a turn. "Melanie, let Kevin give them some food."

"I think I gave them a lot already."

"He won't give them too much. It'll be all right," Mrs. Blake responded.

Melanie reluctantly accepted Mrs. Blake's suggestion. She took a deep breath and passed the container of fish food to Kevin. "Here," she said, placing it in his hand. "Not too much," she cautioned.

Kevin positioned himself closer to the tank and sprinkled the tiny particles of food across the top of the water. Mrs. Blake saw Kevin smile as he watched the fish scrambling through the water competing for the food.

"Look at that one, Jordan!" he said as he pointed at an orange fish with black stripes. "It looks like a tiger fish! Grrrrrrrr . . ." Kevin growled like a tiger. He then put his arm around his little brother and pointed out all the colors of the fish swimming about in the tank. And when he had named every color, he knew it was time for them to go.

"Told ya it would be fun in here," Melanie boasted. "Mrs. Blake's the best teacher in the whole world. There ain't nobody better."

Kevin turned away from the fish tank and focused his attention on Mrs. Blake who had returned to her desk in the front of the room. She was sitting down with her eyes closed and her hands folded. "What's she doin'?" Kevin asked Melanie.

Melanie put her finger to her mouth as though signaling for Kevin to speak softly. "I think she's praying."

"What's she doin' that for?"

"I don't know, but I bet it'll help." Melanie gazed over at Jordan, who still stood silently in front of the fish tank.

"You think she's praying for my brother?"

"She's probably praying for all of us."

"She don't know what we need . . . ," Kevin said a little puzzled.

Melanie looked confident. "Maybe she don't, but God does. Like I said, Mrs. Blake *is* the best teacher in the world. I just guess it's gonna take you a little longer than I thought to see it."

Chapter 3

"PERDEDOR"

THE FIRST FEW WEEKS at Harriet Tubman were un-eventful for Kevin. In fact, if anyone had asked, he would have been quick to describe them as "boring." After that first day, he accepted an invitation from Melanie to sit with her at lunch, but he rarely joined in the conversations with her and her friends. Kevin thought they were too much like him, and the last thing he wanted or needed was more reminders of how he saw himself. If there was one word he could choose to label Melanie and "her crew," as he called them, it was simply the word "obedient."

Looking at them sitting side by side, he told himself it was as if each one of them had been made in "cookie-cutter fashion." They were all so alike; it made Kevin cringe. These were the kids who got good grades without really trying, always turned in their homework assignments on time, and did what they were told without question. They were liked by their teachers and were often the ones picked to do special things like delivering messages to the office and helping with bulletin boards. Sometimes they were even chosen to make the daily morning announcements. Overall, they were privileged and considered the "cream of the crop."

Kevin knew all too well the benefits that came along with good behavior because he had been obedient pretty much every day of his twelve-year-old life. In fact, when he thought about it, he couldn't remember ever being any other way. It was the one comment his teachers often wrote on the back of his report cards: *Kevin is a very nice boy who always does what he is told. He is an excellent example of obedience.*

Thinking about those words and the number of times he'd seen them or heard comments like that made Kevin gasp because no one ever seemed to look beyond the "obedient Kevin" to see if anyone else was there. Rarely was a "good kid" asked if everything was okay. However, the lack of concern was understandable because these were the children who always appeared to "have it all together."

But Kevin was starting to feel like the mold he'd been cast in was beginning to shatter, and he didn't know what he was supposed to do to try and keep it intact. He desperately wanted to tell someone that the boy who so easily came across as "an excellent example of obedience" wasn't perfect the way many of those close around saw him.

At the beginning, he told himself if he tried to do everything right and succeeded, surely he would get noticed. And why wouldn't it work? he wondered. Everyone noticed his little brother for all the things he couldn't do. So why wouldn't Kevin get at least the same attention for the things he could do? To his surprise, he found out that doing things right only made him more invisible. Through his young eyes, he soon realized since less time was needed for him, whatever time was left over was promptly given to Jordan.

In Kevin's desire to do what was right, he was quick to acknowledge Jordan as someone who really needed the extra care. He wanted to tell his mom how he felt but was smart enough to see how full her hands already were in trying to cope with Jordan every day. And when those rare moments came when she finally got a chance to relax, her serenity was usually broken by that all too familiar loud, high-pitched scream that could pierce through walls and break a mother's heart.

Kevin despairingly searched for his share of the attention, but there never seemed to be enough minutes in a day to allow him to successfully carve out his due.

Kevin told himself he would be satisfied just to be able to play with his brother and get the chance to know what it was like to do something special with him. He wanted to draw pictures, climb trees, and skateboard down the sidewalks of their neighborhood. And he wanted to whisper secrets in Jordan's ear that only brothers could share.

It was as if one day Kevin's baby brother stopped babbling and cooing and from that moment on the gleam that filled the toddler's eyes suddenly went away. No longer would he reach with outstretched hands to give hugs to his mother and his big brother and gurgle with laughter when they hugged him back.

It was then that Kevin and everyone who loved him began to watch Jordan begin little by little to slip away. Strangely, it was at that same time Kevin began to disappear too; however, no one noticed at all. All he knew was that he was the bigger brother and that made him determined to do whatever was expected of him when it came to helping Jordan.

Maybe coming to a new school had been the turning point for Kevin. He wasn't sure yet. He did, however, believe that in the short time since he and his brother had come to Harriet Tubman, something was different about both of them. He just didn't know exactly what it was.

Kevin couldn't help but wonder if Mrs. Blake had really prayed for them like Melanie said. And if her prayers reached God's ears, then why couldn't he see it working? Yet at the same time, it appeared that Jordan was learning a little more each day.

He laughed to himself and thought, *Jordan even gets more attention from God than I do.* He was embarrassed about feeling jealous of his little brother. But all he could think about was how tired he was of being "the good kid" because no one, not even God, seemed to understand or recognize that good kids hurt too.

Although she hadn't known Kevin very long, the change in him didn't easily slip past Melanie. After all, recognizing a change in her new friend was just something else she just happened to come across. It was another one of Melanie Clark's "discoveries." Right away, she noticed on some days when Kevin would come for lunch, he just stared at his food. Then after taking only one or two bites, he would throw away his sandwich, sit quietly, and draw for the rest of the lunch period.

Though the daily school lunch menu wasn't a topic she cared to discuss, seeing Kevin look so unhappy about it at least gave her a reason to start a conversation. "Don't like today's lunch, huh?"

"It's okay," he answered but was careful not to look at her.

"I didn't like it either, but I ate most of it anyway. Mrs. Brundidge says, 'if you don't eat, you won't grow and neither will your brain.'"

Melanie waited, figuring Kevin would ask her why she would eat most of something that she didn't like. But he didn't. So she freely gave him an explanation. "And my mom always reminds me about the kids in the world who don't have enough food to eat. So I don't wanna be wasteful."

No matter how hard she tried to get Kevin to talk to her, he offered very little in the way of a response. Except for an "uh huh" or "yeah," she got nothing. And after what she counted to be about three or four attempts, Melanie finally gave up. Something had clearly wedged its way between their friendship.

The more time she spent thinking about it, the more convinced she was that she'd figured out the cause. She could see Kevin surveying an area called "the time-out table." And there sitting at the table was a boy who had been assigned that particular spot for the past two weeks. Melanie shook her head no, trying to deter Kevin's interest, but from the minute he became curious, everything seemed to take a turn for the worse.

On this day, Kevin noticed another boy walk past the table. And when he did, after making sure no one was listening, he said something to the boy who sat alone and then laughed loudly as he walked away. He only said one word, but Kevin didn't know what it meant because the boy had spoken it in Spanish. One thing he did know: whatever the word meant, it made the boy at the table feel bad. There was an obvious look of hurt that showed all over his face.

Breaking out of his self-imposed silence, Kevin spoke. "What's that word mean?" he asked, pestering Melanie for an answer. He knew that she understood some Spanish words because he heard her speaking with her friend Gabriella. This time it was Melanie's turn to ignore him. When she continued talking to the girl in the seat next to her, he decided to ask her again. This time when he tapped her on the arm, he spoke louder. "What's that word mean?"

She reluctantly pulled herself away from her conversation. "What word?"

"PER-DE-DOR, what's it mean?"

"Oh, you mean *perdedor*? Why do you wanna know?" she asked.

"Just tell me!" Kevin demanded.

"Loser," Melanie said purposely lowering her voice. "It means loser."

"And who's that kid over there?" he asked, pointing at the table where the boy sat alone.

Melanie tried to act as though she hadn't heard him, but Kevin was determined to get his question answered. And Melanie was the one to answer it, so he kept up his persistence. This time he gave her arm a little shake to make sure he had her full attention. "That kid over there . . . who is he?"

Before Melanie allowed any more words to come out of her mouth, she frowned with displeasure. "His name is Curtis Givens. And take my word, he's trouble. If you know like I do, you'll stay away from him." She then turned to the girl sitting on her left and continued her conversation. Just then the bell rang, signaling it was time for the day's fifteen-minute recess. It was cool but sunny, so that meant everyone could go outside—even Curtis.

Turning back toward Kevin, Melanie spoke quickly. "Wanna play kick ball?"

"No, you go ahead," he said, declining her invitation.

Melanie got up from the table and threw away her trash. "All right, see ya in class!" She called back and hurried outside with the others.

Kevin waited for a few minutes by the door, just long enough to see Melanie reach the other side of the playground where the kick-ball game had already begun. Once outside, he didn't have to look very far before he found Curtis kneeling down by a tree. He held a stick in his hand and used it to write something in the dirt. Careful to form each letter perfectly, he didn't even notice Kevin standing behind him.

Curtis put all of his concentration into whatever it was he was creating in the dirt. Not wanting to disturb him, Kevin quietly came closer to get a better look. But he couldn't stay quiet very long because his curiosity wouldn't let him.

"What's that?" he asked, leaning down and turning his head on an angle. He was hoping to get a better view. Kevin could tell that Curtis was writing some kind of message because he could partially see the big block style letters he was making. However, as hard as he tried he couldn't make out what it said.

Curtis slightly turned around for only a second. "Nothing," he said as he continued to write.

Kevin tried to be funny, hoping Curtis would laugh. "It's got to be something cause it's there, right?"

This time Curtis didn't bother to turn around. He wasn't

going to let Kevin or anyone else interrupt him.

Kevin wanted to find a stick of his own and try his hand at making some of those fancy letters like the ones Curtis was drawing. He smiled as he bent down right next to Curtis. His face was covered in eagerness. "I can do that," he offered. "Want some help? I can draw pretty good."

"Naw, I'm okay," Curtis said.

Now I know why he don't have any friends, Kevin told himself. *He don't want none.*

Once their conversation ended, Curtis thought Kevin had gone but he was wrong. He had simply stepped away and found a small stick of his own. He bent down and began drawing on a patch of ground on the opposite side of the tree. Making sure he didn't get in Curtis's way, he stayed on his own side. Surprisingly, Curtis didn't yell or tell Kevin to get lost like he was known to do when other kids got too close. In a way, though, what he did was worse because he simply acted like Kevin didn't exist.

Curtis kept drawing until he heard the bell ending recess. He got up, tossed the stick to the side, and began walking back toward the building.

When Kevin saw Curtis get up, he took his foot and smeared the drawing he had started and followed him. "Wanna draw tomorrow?" he called out.

Curtis merely walked away and never glanced back at his would-be friend. Kevin intentionally slowed down his pace so he would no longer be alongside Curtis. He didn't want to bother him. In spite of how hard he tried, his plans to make friends with the boy who seemed to have none had failed.

Kevin couldn't explain why he even cared about wanting to

become friends with someone who, according to Melanie, was nothing but trouble anyway. Maybe it was the common interest they shared when it came to art. Deep down, Kevin sensed that Curtis Givens needed a friend. And somewhere deep down inside of this troubled boy, Curtis really wanted one.

Curtis had already established a reputation for being difficult and extremely hard to get along with. Since his arrival at Harriet Tubman a little more than a year ago, he'd only made one friend, a boy named Vincent Henderson. But when Vincent moved away over the summer, Curtis found himself alone again once school opened in September.

So at thirteen, by no choice of his own, he had become a "loner," spending many of his lunch periods sitting at a table by himself. In most of his classes he was relegated to the back of the room where his teachers collectively believed that to be the only place where he was "less likely to get into trouble."

On her way back inside the building, Melanie stopped where Curtis's drawing remained etched in the ground. She stood staring at each neatly carved and distinct letter in surprise. She realized Curtis hadn't been drawing at all.

"Look," she said, calling for Kevin to come near. Kevin waved his hand as though telling her that he didn't want to be bothered. Melanie knew it was something he needed to see. She ran to catch up with him and, without saying a word, grabbed Kevin by the arm and pulled him back to see Curtis's drawing.

"Look," she said again, pointing at what Curtis had done.

When Kevin read what Curtis had taken so much time to perfect, he couldn't feel anything but sorrow for him. There, in great big, beautiful block style letters, Curtis had used his recess period to create what otherwise may have been seen as a work of art. Instead, there for everyone at Harriet Tubman to see was the word "LOSER" chiseled into the ground.

Suddenly, the words of Alex Martinez took on a sting that was worse than anything that could have been inflicted by the deadliest scorpion. Melanie and Kevin knew that Alex's insults were mean and cruel, but they didn't realize how much real power they held. However, now they saw that Alex's words were becoming dangerous. They were dangerous because it appeared that Curtis Givens was starting to believe them.

Chapter 4

THE LIST

MELANIE WISHED she had been more successful in her attempt to warn Kevin about Curtis. Unfortunately, every time she tried to tell him to stay away from the boy known as "the king of detention," Kevin turned a deaf ear and suggested she mind her own business. It wasn't long after her fifth, and what she decided would be her final, try that Kevin decided to move to a new lunch table in the cafeteria.

So by Monday of his seventh week at Harriet Tubman Elementary, it had become crystal clear that the friendship Kevin once had with Melanie was all but over. He still came to Mrs. Blake's room every day at dismissal time, but only to pick up Jordan and walk him home. One thing he wouldn't do was go inside. He'd stand by the threshold and wait for Mrs. Blake to bring his little brother to the door.

Kevin was always polite and Mrs. Blake was impressed with his good manners. Each day when he arrived, he thanked her and then reached for Jordan's hand. Lately, when the two boys would walk up the ramp and head for the nearest exit, Mrs. Blake watched and wondered about the changes she'd noticed in Kevin as well.

Hoping he would change his mind and decide to come in, she tried standing near her door before he arrived so that she could greet him with a big smile and a friendly hello. Mrs. Blake believed the best medicine for Kevin was for him to join Melanie and Jordan as they worked on puzzles and colored pictures in the back of the room.

If you asked Melanie, she'd tell you that in addition to being the best teacher in the world, Mrs. Blake was the smartest teacher too. She believed she proved her point by acknowledging how resourceful Mrs. Blake was in getting Kevin to come in. She was a wise teacher who knew that letting him make the decision on his own was better than giving him no choice at all. She understood that ordering him inside wouldn't have helped the situation at all. Kevin had to want to come in on his own.

In all her years of teaching, there was one lesson for Mrs. Blake that had stood the test of time. That was the lesson of learning to have patience. She had witnessed many times over just how far a little patience could go. And for the kind of results Mrs. Blake was hoping for, she knew she'd have to pray, wait patiently on God, and have lots of faith.

Even though she didn't know Kevin very well, he seemed more distant now than he had on that first day when Melanie brought him to the room. Mrs. Blake noticed if Melanie was already there when Kevin arrived, the most he would give her in the way of a greeting was a slight wave of his hand. Then he'd quickly turn his head and look away. Melanie suspected Curtis was at fault for the breakup of her friendship with Kevin. She strongly believed in her heart that the changes she saw in Kevin were a direct result of his hanging around Curtis.

Kevin was pleased when all the effort he had put into watching Curtis draw during noontime recess finally paid off. One day after offering to help Curtis with his drawing, he was given a chance to show what he could do.

"Not bad," Curtis said, pointing at the block letters Kevin had carefully and neatly crafted in the dirt. And when he had finished, the one name that always found its way into his thoughts neatly rested on the soft soil before him—"Jordan."

Right away Curtis saw a need to comment. "Ain't that the name of that little kid who can't talk?" he asked him.

Kevin could feel a confrontation about to happen. "Yeah, that's his name," he said, trying to sound tough. "And he *can* talk . . . and . . . he's my brother."

Curtis knew he'd spoken too fast when he saw anger in Kevin's eyes. "I didn't know he was your brother. Can I ask ya something?"

Kevin didn't know what the question was, but he stood ready to defend his little brother at even the slightest hint that Curtis was about to say something insulting. "Go ahead and ask."

Curtis waited a few seconds before venturing to ask his question. "Uh . . . ya brother . . . can he draw?"

Curtis had asked well because he could see Kevin's anger giving way to a pleasant smile. "Naw, he can't draw. But thanks for askin'. Nobody ever does. People just kinda look at him and figure he can't do much of anything."

"Yeah," Curtis said. "Kinda like me."

Kevin looked at Curtis and thought how wrong Melanie was about him. In a way, he wasn't that different from Jordan. No one seemed to think he could do much of anything either.

"Whadda you like to draw?" Kevin asked Curtis.

Kevin could see how enthusiastic Curtis was about sharing his interests.

"Art things!" he said. "I like to draw pictures of vases and jewelry and stuff like that. Like that real old stuff I seen in a museum once."

Not wanting to let Curtis think he knew more about art than he did, Kevin added some details of his own to the conversation.

"Yeah, I seen some of that stuff too. I had a teacher named Mr. Addison last year for social studies and he brought in this big thick art book. It had pictures of pyramids and paintings and everything. One day I'm gonna go and see some of those things."

"Me too," Curtis boasted. "I'm gonna see 'em too."

Since that day when Curtis allowed Kevin to come into his world and share his art, all of Kevin's recess time was spent drawing with his new friend. And except for their mutual artistic giftedness, everything else about them spelled total opposites.

Wondering why Kevin appeared to "look up to Curtis" was a real mystery to Melanie. She had been convinced from the start that their ill-fated association would eventually land Kevin into some kind of trouble. It was strange that no one bothered to ask Kevin why he did everything he could to cultivate a friendship that everyone else believed was doomed and going nowhere.

Nevertheless, Kevin found himself drawn to the likes of Curtis because he was one kid who did what he wanted to do and said what he wanted to say. He never bit his tongue or held back about anything he wanted you to know.

However, on those many occasions when the words spilling out of his mouth came faster than the thoughts creating them, it was easy to predict that some kind of calamity couldn't be far behind. Yet, somehow the Kevin who rarely shared what he really thought about most things admired this seemingly bigger than life classmate who, in the blink of an eye, would say whatever he felt like saying. So the more Kevin hung around Curtis, the more his curiosity was starting to get the better of him. Just once he wanted to know what that kind of freedom felt like to speak his mind like Curtis Givens always did.

Kevin thought if he did have the courage to speak up, the first question he'd ask would be why he had to watch Jordan every day. He wanted some days to belong just to him. For once he wanted the freedom to run off with his friends and not have to worry about making sure his little brother was okay. He didn't think that was too much to ask. In fact, he believed that's what his life would be like if everything was "normal."

So instead of shooting basketballs through a hoop and collecting "high fives" from his friends when he made a shot, Kevin often wondered when he'd find himself in the middle of a fight to defend Jordan because someone had decided to make fun of him. Yes, Kevin had learned all too well how to keep many of his feelings locked up inside.

Curtis, on the other hand, couldn't have been more different. His reputation for being a "bad influence" preceded him, and those who wanted to stay out of trouble stayed away from him. And while he insisted that he was twelve, those who knew him from the year before were well aware this was his second year in sixth grade, so that actually made him thirteen.

Standing at least an inch taller than most of the boys in his class should have given away the fact that Curtis Givens was only masquerading as a "regular" twelve-year-old. He was heavier than most of the other boys too, but this was seen as an advantage when someone was needed to block when the gym class played football.

While Kevin knew Curtis wasn't the best choice for a friend, for now, he was a living example of the kind of courage Kevin wished he had. He believed it took courage for Curtis to act the way he did; especially when he knew what the consequences of his actions would be. Word around the school was that Curtis Givens had spent more time in after-school detention than any other student in the history of Harriet Tubman Elementary School. And if anyone wanted to dispute his one claim to fame, he was more than ready to defend his title.

On this day, it was clear Kevin was ready to make a choice. It was time to remove from his report card forever that "obedient" comment that had followed him so closely from school to school. Mr. Rayner, the language arts teacher, had just asked the class to copy a sentence he had written on the board. Mr. Rayner was known to have somewhat of a reputation of his own. He was the ultimate "no-nonsense" teacher.

When students entered his room, he expected them to be ready to work and to do so quietly. He didn't look kindly upon instigators. And he considered Curtis Givens to be one of the biggest instigators to ever enter the hallowed halls of Harriet Tubman.

No matter how many times Mr. Rayner saw fit to send Curtis on his way to detention, nothing changed. It was like watching the same scene in a movie played over and over again. And the one thing Mr. Rayner promised himself was to never allow even the slightest possibility that a cloned copy of Curtis would ever surface in his classroom.

The class assignment had been given. After writing a sentence on the board, Mr Rayner directed the students to underline the subject part once and the predicate part of the sentence twice. Even though everything inside of him said no, he asked Curtis to go to the board and do the underlining in the example. However, instead of following Mr. Rayner's directions, Curtis began to draw pictures of what the sentence stated.

Right away, the students in the class began laughing at Curtis's antics and that caused Mr. Rayner to give his usual and most predictable response. "Mr. Givens," he bellowed in his baritone voice, "are you trying to get on my list again?" Hearing the word "list" brought all the sounds of laughter to a cold still silence.

Not being one to back down, Curtis stared Mr. Rayner directly in the eye and said, "You mean, there's somebody else's name on it too?"

Mr. Rayner was known to write the names of students who misbehaved in the top left corner of the blackboard. Interestingly enough, the only name that ever seemed to be there was Curtis's.

"One name don't make a list," Curtis protested. "So, if I'm the only name there, you don't have a list." And while technically Curtis was absolutely correct, everyone knew Mr. Rayner was the one teacher you didn't argue with even if your point was well taken. To Curtis's comment, he merely walked over to that portion of the board and made a swift check mark right next to Curtis's name and continued instructing his class in the day's grammar lesson.

Kevin leaned in close to the student sitting next to him and whispered, "What's that mean?"

Checking to make sure his teacher didn't see him, he spoke very fast. "Mr. Rayner don't play like that. It means Curtis just got a detention," he whispered back.

Hearing the very words that most students feared seemingly had no effect on Curtis at all. In fact, he appeared to welcome Mr. Rayner's warning as a challenge. You could almost feel the hairs stand up on the back of some of the students' necks when Curtis had the audacity to raise his hand to ask a question. Mr. Rayner's eyeglasses were on the tip of his nose. Lowering his eyes just enough to give himself a proper focus, he peered down at Curtis.

"Yes, Curtis?" he cautiously inquired.

"Is my detention for today, or can I pick the day I want?"

By the time everyone could hear Curtis's tongue hit against his front teeth to say the letter "t" at the end of the word "want," it was certain he would soon be on his way out the door. At the sound of Curtis's question, Mr. Rayner's whole body seemed to stiffen as he turned himself around and walked back to his desk.

Without blinking an eye, he grabbed his red pen and hurriedly scribbled something on a notepad. When he was done, he snatched the piece of paper off the pad, folded the note, and walked it over to Curtis. Placing it on the desk, he pointed at the door. He said, "please take this, Mr. Givens, and leave!"

Curtis put on a brave face. But there was something about the way he slowly got up from his seat and walked away. There was hesitation in each step he took on his way to the door. It was as if he was sending a message that said if he had it to do all over again, maybe he would have tried harder to keep his mouth closed. But he knew it was too late. He could have apologized and asked Mr. Rayner for another chance. However, knowing if the shoe had been on the other foot, he'd stick to his guns, make Mr. Rayner accept his fate, and not listen to any protest.

Every eye in the room followed him as he left to go to the one place in the building where his face was as familiar as Mrs. Gaines, the school nurse. He was on his way to the principal's office. And just like all the other times, he could expect a lecture, a call home to his mother, and a bright pink detention slip.

The minute the classroom door closed separating Curtis from his classmates, the students in Mr. Rayner's class went back to work. Kevin had an expression on his face that looked like admiration for Curtis's boldness. He didn't seem bothered by the fact that Curtis's behavior had obviously been to his own detriment.

When Mr. Rayner's back was turned, the boy in the seat next to Kevin quickly tossed a note onto his desk. Kevin's eyes moved carefully about the room following Mr. Rayner's footsteps. He was intent on making sure not to open the note until the time was exactly right. And when he knew the moment had come, he hurried to unfold it. It simply said the words, "See what I mean?" It was signed "Melanie."

Kevin glanced over at Melanie, whose seat was on the other side of the room, and sent her a signal. He took her note and crumpled it into a small ball. She, in turn, got his message loud and clear and looked away.

Then Kevin did something that let Melanie know, without a doubt, that he was about to cross the very clear line that Mr. Rayner had established regarding his expectations for students' behavior in his class. Kevin waited until it was so quiet that a straight pin could have been dropped and heard when it hit the floor. When he saw that Mr. Rayner's back was turned, he took his elbow and nudged his thick grammar book to the edge of his desk, giving it just the amount of force it needed until it hit the floor hard.

Wham! was the sound it made and instantly every head turned around to see who'd dare make the mistake of creating that kind of disturbance in Mr. Rayner's classroom.

Mr. Rayner was as startled by the commotion as the students. He turned around to see what had happened. But before he could ask any questions, he noticed Kevin's face was wearing a sly grin. When their eyes met, he said, "guess my book fell."

Mr. Rayner still considered Kevin a new student at Harriet Tubman so he tried to give him the benefit of the doubt. "Please try and keep your book on the desk, Kevin," he said jokingly. "I wouldn't want your name to end up on my list too."

Melanie could feel herself getting nervous and immediately prayed that Kevin would do the "smart thing" and say nothing. But before she could say "amen," it was already too late.

"But you don't have a list," Kevin said. "You only have one name up there and one name don't make it a list."

"Uh oh," Melanie whispered. She cringed at the thought of what was about to happen.

THE LIST

Mr. Rayner walked over to that portion of the blackboard that was reserved for students who didn't follow the rules and in all capital letters he wrote, "KEVIN MANNING" directly under Curtis's name. "Now, Mr. Manning," he said sternly, "I have a list and you're on it. I'll see you this afternoon in room 101 for detention."

Chapter 5

DETENTION 101

LATER THAT AFTERNOON, Kevin reluctantly joined the rest of the students who'd been assigned detention in room 101. The whole idea of having to go to detention was new to Kevin, and he wondered if there was a sound explanation for why the same kids had a tendency to come back over and over again. Nothing about the room looked inviting. In fact, with its bare beige walls and old worn-out desks, the feeling he got stepping across its threshold was just the opposite of what he'd felt in Mrs. Blake's room.

Surely, if Kevin had a chance to rethink what had happened in Mr. Rayner's class, he wouldn't have given in to his nagging curiosity and kept his remarks to himself. There was no choice but to complete the detention and do whatever needed to be done in order to make sure he'd never find himself in that place again.

Mr. Dunn, also known as the "detention teacher,"

commanded absolute silence for the total thirty-minute period. And while Kevin had no intention of invoking Mr. Dunn's legendary wrath, he couldn't picture any self-respecting sixth-grader sitting in silence for a full thirty minutes. He also knew better than to show up later than the official scheduled time.

The word around school was if anyone made the mistake of knocking on the door of room 101 even one minute later than the 3:05 p.m. deadline, Mr. Dunn would quickly sign you up for another detention to be served the following day.

Kevin made it inside the room by the skin of his teeth. Just as he arrived, Mr. Dunn was closing the door. So he made it in by only seconds. Just as he was about to head to a seat in the front of the room, he saw Curtis sitting in a corner all the way in the back. He figured if he was going to be in detention, he might as well sit near someone who could tell a good joke and be funny if the need arose.

But under Mr. Dunn's watchful eye, Kevin never got the chance to get anywhere near Curtis. The first sign was when he cleared his throat. "Hmmph! right here," he said, pointing at Kevin while at the same time tapping on the desk next to where he was standing in front of the room. "You can sit here."

Kevin could tell that showing any signs of protesting Mr. Dunn's direction was a mistake. And it was a good thing he didn't try it. The second he sat down, he saw Mr. Rayner peering through the window and holding a white sheet of paper. His eyes took stock of every student he could see, all the while noting the names of the ones he had personally assigned.

On the sheet of paper he held in his hand, he quickly checked off the names he was responsible for. He had no trouble seeing

Kevin, but was having difficulty seeing Curtis positioned all the way in the back. He stretched his neck as far as he could but that didn't help. So he decided to tap on the window in hopes of getting Mr. Dunn's attention. As soon as he got the official "thumbs-up," he knew his question had been answered. After getting Mr. Dunn's signal, he made one last swift check mark next to Curtis's name and he was on his way.

Realizing he was facing at least twenty-nine minutes of silence, Kevin began wondering if trying to be the "new funny guy" in class had been worth what he'd bargained for. Shaking his head as though listening to a lecture taking place inside his own brain, he quietly opened his math book and took out a sheet of paper to begin his homework. If nothing else, he figured he could get a jump start on that day's homework assignment. But just like finding out that the seat in the back of the room was off limits, so too was the thought of getting any homework done.

Once the door was closed, Mr. Dunn went into his top desk drawer, pulled out an egg timer and set it for exactly thirty minutes.

"Today's detention assignment is as follows," he announced, pointing to the blackboard. "Those ten vocabulary words are to be listed in alphabetical order, defined along with its part of speech, used in your own sentences, with each word underlined. I will be checking your work for proper usage and correct punctuation."

Mr. Dunn continued issuing his instructions, "And should you have the misfortune of coming back tomorrow because you didn't do the assignment correctly, you will rewrite everything I find misspelled, incorrectly punctuated, or sloppily written. Does everyone understand?"

Although he didn't need to wait for anyone to answer his

question, Mr. Dunn's eyes scanned every face in the room to make sure. The wall-to-wall silence in the room spoke volumes.

He then called up one row of students at a time and handed each one a dictionary and two sheets of lined paper. For a few seconds, Kevin stared at the vocabulary list. And while careful not to let any words slip out that anyone could hear, he moved his lips as he labored to pronounce each one. When Mr. Dunn called Kevin's row to come up, he closed his math book, returned it to his book bag, and fell in line with the others waiting to receive the dictionary and paper needed to do the assignment.

One thing Kevin noticed was that Curtis had a whole lot less to say in Mr. Dunn's detention than he did in Mr. Rayner's class. In this room, he wasn't the wisecracking, loud-talking kid that Kevin had tried to imitate. In detention, he was just like everyone else. He wanted to get finished with his written work and probably hoped he'd never have to return to room 101 again.

Unfortunately, no matter how much Curtis may have wanted to stay away, his detention schedule had become somewhat of a joke among the students at Tubman. Whatever his wish may have been about wanting this to be his last time, it was predictable that before the week was over, he'd be back. And to prove it, when the thirty minutes were up, he placed his work on Mr. Dunn's desk and returned his dictionary to the shelf. Before Curtis walked away, Kevin thought he heard Mr. Dunn pleasantly say, "see you tomorrow."

As Curtis slowly walked to the nearest exit door, Kevin tried to catch up with him. "Hey, wait up!" he called. Curtis never stopped but only turned slightly to see who was calling him. When he recognized that it was Kevin, he kept walking. But that only made Kevin walk faster. When he finally caught up with Curtis, he wanted to know how he was able to complete his work so quickly.

"How'd you finish all that work?"

"I didn't. I drew a picture and put it on his desk. That's why he said, 'see you tomorrow.'"

Kevin realized what he thought he'd heard was right. And from where he stood, it appeared Curtis was determined to be a "detention regular," just like Melanie had warned. Now the mystery surrounding the question of why he had the reputation at Harriet Tubman for having served the most detentions ever had been solved.

Kevin knew it was none of his business, but he wondered about Curtis's choice not to do the work just the same. He allowed his interest to win out over his common sense and found himself blurting out the one question he figured all sixth-grade inquiring minds wanted to know: "Why don't you just do the work and get it over with?" he asked boldly.

Curtis stopped and met Kevin eye to eye with one of the most serious looks that he could ever remember seeing on someone his age. "Because I like to draw, and Mr. Dunn gives me paper every day."

Kevin said to himself, "I like drawing too, but I ain't willing to spend every day after school doing detention assignments just to get clean sheets of paper." He couldn't understand why anyone would.

Curtis knew how much Kevin liked drawing too. "You draw too, don't ya?"

Kevin was eager to say yes hoping that during the next recess period the two of them could draw together. But there was something peculiar about the way Curtis looked when he asked the question. It was as if he already knew the answer. However, somewhere in back of his question, there was a plan in motion that he wasn't ready to reveal.

"Yeah, let me show ya." Kevin pulled his notebook out of his book bag and flipped to the pages in the back. He could tell Curtis liked the drawings because his serious look disappeared. He knew Curtis Givens was impressed.

"Ever do big art?"

"A lotta times," Kevin answered not wanting to give the impression that he was clueless.

"If you meet me tomorrow after school, I'll show you how to draw some *real big art*."

"What about Mr. Dunn? Don't you have to go to his deten—?"

Curtis interrupted. "Not if I can stay in all my classes and not get sent to the office. If I'm not sent to detention, then I don't haffta go."

Kevin found himself excited at the thought of getting a chance to draw and finding a friend who liked art as much as he did. In addition to his reputation for being disruptive in class most of the time, Curtis was also acknowledged as perhaps the finest artist in the whole sixth grade. And Kevin wasn't about to pass up an opportunity to draw with him.

Making sure Curtis knew he had no reservations, he readily spoke up. "Count me in. I'll be there."

Kevin could see Melanie coming out of Mrs. Blake's room and turned around, hoping to avoid her and her unwelcome advice.

"Mrs. Blake's lookin' for you!" she yelled.

Without looking in her direction, Kevin raced to Mrs. Blake's room to pick up his little brother. He could still hear Melanie scolding him about the importance of being on time as she continued walking in the opposite direction. When Kevin reached Mrs. Blake's classroom, he could tell that she was displeased about his tardiness.

But before she got a chance to express her dissatisfaction, Kevin formally apologized. "I'm sorry, Mrs. Blake. I was . . ."

"You were in detention. Melanie told me."

Kevin didn't say another word. He could read the disappointment in Mrs. Blake's eyes. And at the mention of his "former" friend's name, Kevin felt himself getting mad. He planned to tell her what he thought of her tomorrow, but just as quickly he convinced himself to say nothing to her at all. He knew that he'd managed to get himself into enough trouble for one day and thought maybe staying away from her was the best thing he could do. This way, Melanie wouldn't get the satisfaction of saying, "I told you so."

Kevin could see Jordan sitting in a chair at the back table playing with a little red truck. He rolled it back and forth continuously. It wasn't until Kevin placed his hand on the truck to make it stop that the wheels were finally stilled. Stopping the toy truck caused Jordan to turn and see Kevin standing next to him. Jordan looked at him, but said nothing. Then he reached for the truck and shrieked when Kevin wouldn't return it.

"NO, JORDAN!" Kevin said loudly as he lifted his brother out of the chair. "It's time to go home." Kevin was surprised that Jordan didn't put up more of a fuss. He wasn't kicking his legs or wildly waving his arms like he was known to do. But just the same, as Kevin took him by the hand, he could feel his little brother tightening up all over. He leaned in close to his brother's ear and whispered, "c'mon." Then making sure he held Jordan's hand gently, he told him, "let's go home."

Jordan's eyes widened as though he had a whole lot to say but yet said nothing. It was as if Kevin could tell a story by looking into his little brother's eyes. He believed Jordan wanted to say how happy he was to see his "big brother" and tell him all about how good his day had been in Mrs. Blake's class.

So the very words that Jordan failed to say, Kevin imagined into existence. He had trained himself to have good thoughts and sometimes he pretended that he could read the ones going on inside his little brother's brain. Hanging on to the brotherly scene he'd conjured up, Kevin stopped, kneeled down, and lovingly tied Jordan's shoelaces. "There ya go, now we can leave."

Kevin took Jordan by the hand and led him toward the front of Mrs. Blake's room. He saw Mrs. Blake sitting at her desk and hoped she wouldn't ask him why he hadn't come back after his first visit. He'd almost made it to the door, having successfully gotten one foot over the threshold, when Mrs. Blake called him. "You haven't been back," she said, pointing at Kevin and wearing a surprised look. "We've missed you."

Maybe, Kevin thought, *Mrs. Blake is the one who is a real mind reader.* Clearing his throat, he said, "Me and Melanie, we aren't friends anymore, so I . . . "

"You're always welcome to stop by and visit," she assured him.

Kevin was relieved to find that Mrs. Blake still welcomed him even though his friendship with Melanie had ended. "Thank you, Mrs. Blake."

"I'll see you tomorrow, Jordan," she said softly. "And I hope we'll see you too, Kevin."

Suddenly, Jordan raised his hand just as Mrs. Blake had done. He pointed his finger and repeated the word "you."

This time it was Kevin's eyes that widened with excitement. A new word had come out of Jordan! Kevin was beginning to think there was truly something wonderful and special about Mrs. Blake and her beautiful, colorful classroom.

"Jordan is working hard and he is learning," Mrs. Blake announced. Kevin could see and hear in Mrs. Blake's declaration that she was just as happy about Jordan speaking as he was.

He was anxious to find out what else his brother could do. "Can he say something else?"

Before Mrs. Blake had a chance to answer him, Kevin turned to Jordan and asked his question again. "Say somethin' else?" he pleaded as he waited for another word to come forth. But when his brother slightly lowered his head, he knew he had seen and heard the one miracle with Jordan's name on it for the day.

"Thank you, Mrs. Blake," he said, carefully leading Jordan toward the door. "I won't be late again."

"Maybe you'll come by tomorrow and help with the fish?" It was as if the invitation was a special peace offering. Kevin wondered if Mrs. Blake had already forgotten that he'd just told her that he wasn't friends with Melanie anymore. And he was afraid if he reminded her, maybe she would take back the invitation. He decided, however, to be honest and tell her again.

"Uh, Mrs. Blake," he said, rubbing the right side of his forehead. "Me and Melanie aren't friends anymore."

"I see," she said, folding her arms and taking a minute to

think. "Well, please know that you're both welcome to stop in anyway, all right?"

"Thanks, Mrs. Blake." Kevin waited a couple of minutes while trying to get up enough courage to ask her an all-important question. "If I come, can Curtis come too?"

"Who?" she was quick to ask.

Kevin couldn't understand why she seemed so surprised. Surely she must have heard that his new friend was Curtis, "the detention king." In fact, he suspected Mrs. Blake had heard all about his new friendship. There was no way Melanie hadn't shared everything she knew. And Kevin was pretty sure Mrs. Blake knew who Curtis was anyway. Everybody at Harriet Tubman knew the name Curtis Givens. But when he heard her answer, Kevin began thinking maybe she didn't.

"Sure, it's fine," she continued. "Bring him along."

Finding out that his friend was welcome made Kevin more at ease with the idea of going to Mrs. Blake's room after school. "Sure . . . I'll . . . I mean, we'll come."

Mrs. Blake could tell Kevin had something else on his mind and tried to give him an opportunity to tell her what he was thinking. However, when he picked up his brother's lunch box and started walking toward the door, she decided to ask a question of her own. "Is everything all right, Kevin?"

"I wanted to know if I come tomorrow, if you'd still let me feed the fish." Kevin could already anticipate the word yes falling off of Mrs. Blake's tongue, but when he heard her real answer, it startled him a bit.

"If you can bring me a note from Mr. Rayner letting me

know you were on your best behavior in his class, then I'll say yes to your request. Is that a deal?"

The first thought that came to Kevin's mind was, *Now I'm absolutely sure Melanie talked too much. Only she could have told Mrs. Blake about what happened in Mr. Rayner's class earlier today.* She knew that Kevin's behavior had landed him in detention. However, since he had no plans of ever going back there, he considered the terms Mrs. Blake offered fair and easy so he immediately jumped at the proposition.

"Okay. I'll bring the note," he cheerfully agreed.

"Then I'll see you here tomorrow afternoon. And, Jordan," she said, taking his small hand in hers, "I'll see you tomorrow morning."

As Kevin led Jordan out of the room, Mrs. Blake said goodbye to Jordan. Kevin noticed that she did so as though she expected Jordan to respond. He didn't, but Mrs. Blake smiled at both of them just the same.

When he and Jordan were in the hall, Kevin pointed at himself and said, "me." Then he pointed at his little brother and said, "you." And Jordan pointed at Kevin and said, "you." Kevin hugged him tightly and led his little brother down the hall and out the door.

Then, a moment later, he glanced back and saw Mrs. Blake still watching. *Melanie might be right about one thing*, Kevin thought. *Maybe Mrs. Blake is the best teacher in the world . . . maybe she is.*

Chapter 6

FOLLOW THE LEADER

BY 3:15 P.M. the next day, Kevin had already broken his promise to Mrs. Blake. He hadn't been assigned detention again, but he hadn't been able to get the note telling of his good behavior from Mr. Rayner either. He thought he was very close until Mr. Rayner said, "one missing homework assignment and too much talking out of turn for one day."

Once he realized there was no chance of getting the note, he saw no reason to show up since he hadn't been able to keep his end of the agreement. Instead, he found himself meeting up with Curtis to take him up on his offer to do some of that "big art" he had bragged about the day before.

Melanie didn't know the particulars of the plan, but when she saw Kevin and Curtis walking down the hall together, she tried to catch up with him in hopes of changing his mind. But Kevin saw her and quickly maneuvered his way through the crowded hallway like a receiver headed for a winning touchdown. He swerved and easily edged his way through all the heavy end-of-the-day traffic.

Melanie realized she wasn't going to get the chance to try and convince him that he was about to make a huge mistake when suddenly Kevin was gone from sight. She wanted to tell him that he would have a better time in Mrs. Blake's room, but he wasn't there to hear what she had to say. Worried about someone she still considered to be a friend, she headed down the corridor alone.

By the time she got to Mrs. Blake's room, Melanie could see her sitting at the back table helping Jordan. She was obviously anxious to join them.

"Hello, Mrs. Blake! Hi, Jordan!" she said as she gently tapped him on his left shoulder. Melanie really liked working with Jordan and helping him. In her mind, he was like one of those great discoveries she was forever talking about. Every time he learned something new, it was like opening a special surprise and never being disappointed.

"Hi, Melanie," Mrs. Blake responded cheerfully. "Is Kevin on his way?"

"I don't think so. I saw him, but he was going in another direction with Curtis Givens."

Mrs. Blake tried not to look concerned, but Melanie could tell she didn't feel good about what she heard. "Oh, I see," she said. Mrs. Blake didn't ask or say anything else about Kevin. It was as if hearing the news that he and Curtis had chosen not to come was more than she wanted to know. There was an uneasy feeling about this new friendship Kevin had somehow initiated.

"Okay," she said, lightly tapping Jordan on the arm. Let's

get back to work." Mrs. Blake resumed stacking colored blocks and handing them to Jordan while prompting him to do the same. Each time she gave him a block, she named its color.

"Blue," she said as she gave him the blue one. She repeated each color over and over again, hoping that Jordan would do the same. After hearing the word six times in a row, she found herself greeted with a softly spoken response. "B-l-u-e," Jordan slowly repeated.

"Boy, Mrs. Blake, that's kinda like that game, 'Follow the Leader!' May I try?" Melanie asked. "Please, Mrs. Blake, may I try?"

Mrs. Blake passed the blocks to Melanie who quickly sat down next to Jordan. "Not too fast. Okay, Melanie?"

"Okay."

Melanie smiled at Jordan whose eyes followed the yellow rectangular block she held in her hand.

"Yellow," she said. "It's yellow." She placed the block on the table in front of him and pointed. "Yellow," she said again. "Yellow."

Jordan reached for the block but did not repeat the word. He picked it up, briefly held it in his hand, and then let it drop on the table.

"That's okay," Melanie told him while picking up another block. She was careful to be patient with him in just the way she'd seen Mrs. Blake work with him.

"You do what I do. Okay, Jordan?" Melanie announced joyfully.

Seeing that Jordan was in the hands of a very capable helper, Mrs. Blake got up and returned to her desk.

"Mrs. Blake, when we're done, may I feed the fish?"

"Yes, Melanie, you can but not until you've shown Jordan all of the colors, all right?"

"All right!" Melanie immediately went to work, showing Jordan the blocks and telling him each color. Though he didn't repeat any of them, Melanie wasn't discouraged. She continued presenting the blocks one at a time and smiled brightly each time she did.

Suddenly the serene moments they were enjoying were disturbed when Mrs. Kramer, the principal's secretary, appeared at Mrs. Blake's door. Mrs. Kramer, known for her quiet and usual calm demeanor, wasn't at all like herself when she rushed into the room with her hands shaking wildly as she spoke with Mrs. Blake.

Melanie stopped and turned around to see what all the commotion was about. Although a bit calmer now, Mrs. Kramer was still motioning with her hands a lot. The serious mood hovering over Mrs. Blake's classroom made Melanie feel uneasy. And the more she heard of the two women's conversation, the more uncomfortable she felt.

"Are you sure it was them?" she heard Mrs. Blake ask.

"No doubt at all," Mrs. Kramer declared. "The two of them were caught red-handed." When Melanie heard the phrase "two of them," and saw Mrs. Kramer nod her head yes, she knew what she had hoped wouldn't happen, *had* happened. And while she didn't know any of the details yet, she was pretty sure that somehow Curtis had managed to get Kevin into trouble. The only question left to be answered was—how much trouble?

As soon as Mrs. Kramer left, Melanie could hear the urgency

in Mrs. Blake's voice. Now she spoke in a tone that was very somber and serious.

"Melanie, I want you and Jordan to come with me right now. And please bring his things. You'll be dismissed from the main office."

If Melanie had any doubts, she didn't any longer. It was apparent that both Kevin and Curtis had done something pretty awful, and Principal Tate had summoned for Mrs. Blake to come to his office. Melanie knew this wasn't the time to ask any questions. She did exactly as she was told.

Grabbing her book bag and coat, she picked up Jordan's lunch box and jacket and led him out the door directly behind Mrs. Blake. Mrs. Blake was moving so fast, it was hard for Melanie and Jordan to keep up. They hurried as quickly as they could while trudging up the long ramp that separated the kindergarten wing from the area of the building where the main office was located.

Once they entered the office, Mrs. Blake pointed at a long lime-green leather seat and directed Melanie and Jordan to sit down and not move. Then she gave three light knocks on the door that said "Principal" and stepped inside. Mrs. Blake remained inside the principal's office for at least twenty minutes.

When she finally came out, the mystery of what had happened was over. Along with Mrs. Blake and Principal Tate, out stepped Curtis, Kevin, and Mr. Garrett, the custodian. Both boys hung their heads and stood quietly waiting and hoping someone would tell them that they could leave.

Mr. Tate's voice was hard and firm. "I hope you boys are clear about everything I said in there, because if something like this ever happens again, you'll both be suspended for ten days and a formal complaint will be filed with the authorities. Do you both understand?"

Though he couldn't prove it, Kevin swore he never saw the stern principal blink his eyes the whole time he spoke. He was, however, very certain about one thing—Mr. Tate meant business. A two-week detention had been assigned to both Curtis and Kevin, and if they missed showing up for even one day—they faced instant suspension. Both boys shook their heads yes letting Mr. Tate know that they clearly understood him.

Just as Kevin and Curtis turned to leave, Mr. Tate felt the need to remind them one more time. "You two make sure you report to Mrs. Blake's room at exactly 3:05 p.m. *sharp* for the next two weeks!" The way he yelled the word sharp made Kevin nervous, causing him to silently promise himself to be sure and get there on time.

"We will, Mr. Tate," Curtis said.

Kevin couldn't understand how, after trying so hard to avoid going back to Mrs. Blake's room, he now found himself faced with the reality of spending his detention time there for the next two weeks. Suddenly he understood what people meant when they said, "like pouring salt into a wound," because before he or Curtis had a chance to leave, Mrs. Kramer handed each of them a sealed, white envelope. She instructed the boys to take the notes directly home and give them to their parents. By the firmness of her voice, one could easily tell that the contents of the envelopes could only represent one thing—more trouble.

Kevin took Jordan by the hand; he was more than ready to go. Just as the boys were about to leave the office, Melanie gave

Kevin some startling news that made him understand his peculiar detention placement.

"I forgot to tell ya," she said. "Mrs. Blake's not just the best teacher at Harriet Tubman, she's the vice principal too."

Once they were all outside, Curtis stood by the side of the entrance and signaled for Kevin to come near. Kevin still didn't exactly see Melanie as a friend, but since he needed her to do him a favor, he spoke politely. "Melanie, can you watch Jordan for a minute?"

Melanie thought about his request and remembered how badly Kevin had been treating her lately. She could feel the word "no" right on the tip of her tongue, but she really liked Jordan a lot, and his cute little round face made her heart melt. Melanie told herself if she could have a little brother of her own, she'd choose Jordan in a heartbeat. Looking over at him while he repeatedly swung his right leg back and forth, she found herself agreeing to Kevin's request.

"Oh, all right," she said. "But only for a minute."

"Thanks," Kevin told her as he hurried over to where Curtis was standing.

Curtis stared at Kevin as though trying to read his mind. "Why'd ya do it?"

"Do what?" Kevin asked.

"Why'd ya let Mr. Tate think you did that drawin' on the wall?"

"Cause I had a feelin' you were gonna get in real bad trouble . . . probably more trouble than you did if Mr. Tate knew you had done all that drawin' by yourself," Kevin explained.

"You're right, I woulda. But that still wasn't no reason for you to take the blame. It was my idea, ya know."

"Yeah, I know." Kevin turned to leave but then turned around. "But I didn't have to follow you. I coulda said no and maybe you wouldna taken out that marker and wrote nothing on the wall in the first place."

"Yeah, and maybe I woulda done it anyway," Curtis said, waiting for Kevin to react.

"And maybe you wouldna done it at all," Kevin responded. He could tell Curtis was thinking.

"Maybe you're right," he admitted. "Maybe I wouldna."

"I gotta go," Kevin said. "See ya tomorrow. Remember, no later than 3:05 p.m."

"Maybe I'll show up and maybe I won't," Curtis said.

And there it was again—that flair for sarcasm that Curtis had a way of using to impress those around him. Unfortunately, it was his knack for letting his mouth get him into trouble that often made the other kids stay away. Kevin thought how strange it was that Curtis often didn't know when to keep quiet, while his brother, Jordan, rarely spoke at all.

"Oh, I'll be there," Curtis said, walking off in a huff.

"Why do you bother with him?" Melanie asked.

"He's not so bad," Kevin said, attempting to defend his friend.

"Nothing but bad news," Melanie said with a disapproving tone. "Right, Jordan?"

"You ever seen him draw? He's really good!" Kevin exclaimed.

"But at everything else, he's really bad!" Melanie responded.

Melanie didn't want to talk about Curtis anymore. "You

gonna tell your folks what happened?" She could see her question had reminded Kevin that his very difficult day was far from over.

"I'm gonna let 'em read the note first."

"Guess you're gonna be in a lotta trouble when you get home, huh?"

Kevin hung his head as though ashamed. "Yeah . . . I am."

Melanie felt sorry for Kevin and decided not to mention anything else about what had happened. She just hoped he had learned his lesson where Curtis Givens was concerned. At least she hoped he now knew enough to stay away from him once the two week's detention was over.

Guess we just gotta wait and see, she thought to herself. "Yep, we just gotta wait and see," she said out loud.

IT'S A GOOD THING!

AS A SIXTH-GRADER, Kevin was fully aware that he was supposed to be able to distinguish right from wrong and good from bad. Wrong, of course, was anything that could land him on the receiving end of a two-week detention. Wrong was making the mistake of deciding to take part in a plan to create "big art" on the walls of the boys' washroom and watching Curtis get caught with a permanent black marker in his hand. Right was feeling good about getting commended for achieving the highest math grade in class for the second time on a chapter test. And right was also in knowing that he'd played a part in one of Jordan's accomplishments.

But even in considering all of this, Kevin quietly had to admit to himself that it had been a long time since he heard someone say to him, "well done." That kind of news now seemed like nothing more than a distant memory.

As far as Melanie was concerned, all of Kevin's problems at Harriet Tubman started the day he decided that he wanted Curtis Givens as a friend. In her opinion, their friendship was anything but good. However, Kevin didn't share those feelings. Somehow, in spite of the awful trouble he'd managed to get into, he still believed being a friend to Curtis was the right thing to do.

On his way to detention in Mrs. Blake's classroom, Kevin remembered how she had played soft, soothing music with instruments that sang melodies while he, Melanie, and Jordan stood gazing at the beautiful tropical fish swimming the length of the tank in the back of her room. He was pretty sure Curtis wasn't going to like the music and probably wouldn't like the fish either. Knowing that made Kevin wonder if he should pretend he felt the same way.

Then he thought about the warning Mr. Tate had given. And though he wanted to wait for Curtis, he decided not to take the chance. Kevin was determined he wasn't going to allow himself to be late. He liked Curtis, and greatly admired his artistic talent, but Kevin's mind was made up. No one was going to cause him to get on Mr. Tate's bad side or push him in any deeper than the trouble he was already in.

Just as he was about to turn the corner of the sixth-grade wing, he could hear Curtis's voice. "Hey, Kevin!" he yelled. "Wait up!"

Kevin waved but he kept walking. He figured if Curtis was serious about getting to Mrs. Blake's room on time, he'd just have to move a little faster. And move faster is exactly what he did. Within seconds, he had made his way through the throngs of students coming from every direction and soon found himself walking right beside Kevin. "So, what can you tell me?" Curtis asked anxiously.

Kevin didn't understand Curtis's question. " . . . about what?" he asked.

"Mrs. Blake. Is she nice or is she going to dump a whole lotta work on us 'cause of what we did?"

Kevin kept walking. The more he thought about all the times Curtis had been assigned detention, a part of him couldn't believe that Curtis didn't understand that this one from Mr. Tate was a gift. And, it was a gift that he needed to be grateful about. Kevin cut a glance at Curtis and shook his head in disbelief. Did he actually think there was a way to get around this? For a minute he thought, *Maybe Melanie was right about Curtis being nothing but trouble.*

But, in spite of all the negative things he could easily list to give him reason to stay away from Curtis, Kevin had a hard time ignoring the fact that Curtis possessed artistic talent like nothing he'd ever seen. Perhaps it was the chance he saw to learn and "soak in" some of the giftedness he recognized in such an unlikely friend.

"Whatever she gives us to do, we do it!" Kevin snapped. "I don't want to get in no more trouble. Detention's nothing compared to the trouble I was in when I got home." Kevin's tone sent a clear message. This time he was going to do the right thing. He was no longer going to be "a follower."

For the first time since they had been talking, Curtis seemed interested in what Kevin had to say. "Did ya get hit or something?"

"No, but TV's out for the next two weeks. And to me, that's worse than gettin' hit."

Curtis smiled, but it was a strange kind of smile. It wasn't a smile of enjoyment but one that seemed to say he wished he was in Kevin's place.

"What? You don't think that's bad?" Kevin asked him. "What happened to you when you got home?"

Curtis quickly positioned himself to walk a little bit ahead of Kevin. "The same thing that always happens," he answered with a note of sadness in his voice. "Nothin'."

By the time they reached the classroom door, Curtis had changed his mind about what to expect during Mrs. Blake's detention. "You're right," he said, patting Kevin's shoulder. "Whatever she gives us to do, we do it."

Neither of them went inside right away. Instead they had a perfect view of the entire room as they stood in the doorway. They were greeted by the sounds of soft classical music playing and wondered why. It was something that was unusual to them, but the tones were smooth and melodic and seemed to give the atmosphere around the room a peaceful aura.

They couldn't see Mrs. Blake but easily spotted Melanie sitting at the back table with Jordan. She was showing him some brightly colored blocks with letters painted on the sides of each one. Kevin could tell that Jordan had found a good friend in Melanie. And he could sense how she really cared and wanted to help him. Seeing how well she worked with Jordan made Kevin feel guilty about treating her so badly.

Although Kevin wouldn't have admitted it earlier, he secretly liked Mrs. Blake's classroom. He clearly understood that he and Curtis were there for detention. But, somewhere down deep on the inside, he already knew that when it was over, he would miss going to her room each day.

"Hey," Curtis said pointing. "Ain't that your brother?"

Kevin pretended not to hear Curtis, hoping he wasn't about to say something he'd have to make him regret. But Curtis was just as determined to make sure Kevin heard him.

"That's him, right? . . . back there at the table with Melanie."

Kevin could feel one of those comments getting ready to make its way out of Curtis's mouth. He was probably going to ask why Jordan acts the way that he does. And why he doesn't talk like everybody else. Gifted artist or not, Kevin was not about to let Curtis or anyone else get away with making fun of his little brother.

He dropped his book bag to the floor and stepped so close to Curtis that he couldn't have been more than an inch and a half away from his face. Looking him squarely in the eye, and forming both of his hands into fists, he challenged him. "You got something to say about him?" Kevin demanded.

"About what?" Curtis asked.

"You know what I mean, about my brother," Kevin pressed.

Curtis suddenly found himself face-to-face with "the protector." He could see that Jordan's big brother, Kevin, was ready at a word's notice to defend his younger brother's honor. And Curtis didn't want to run the risk of saying the wrong thing. He often acted tough and tried to give the impression it didn't matter that he had no friends.

But the last thing he wanted to happen was to lose his friendship with Kevin. No matter how he may have come across to others around him, he liked having someone to talk to, someone who liked drawing as much as he did. "I wasn't gonna say nothin' bad about your brother," Curtis responded.

Kevin knew what he was hearing was Curtis's best attempt at offering an apology. So he decided it was good enough and accepted it. "It's okay," he said.

Curtis looked relieved to know everything was all right.

Mrs. Blake was in the small supply closet in the back of the room. She came out because she could hear Kevin and Curtis outside her classroom door. She checked to see what time it was by the clock on the wall and beamed a warm smile the way she was known to do. Looking at the boys and signaling for them to come in, she announced, "Let's get started."

"Are we gonna have to listen to that music playin' the whole time?" Curtis asked her.

Knowing that the two of them had just agreed to do whatever Mrs. Blake told them to do, hearing Curtis's question caused Kevin to stare at his friend in amazement.

"Don't you like the music, Curtis?" Mrs. Blake questioned.

"It ain't that . . . it's just . . . so different. What's it called anyway?"

"Mozart," she said pleasantly.

Mrs. Blake could see a frown forming on Curtis's face. "Well, how about it if you give the music a chance? If it interferes with your assignment, then I'll consider turning it off. Fair enough?" she reasoned.

Curtis figured it was an honorable agreement and shook his head yes. He very quietly nudged Kevin in the arm and whispered, "Don't know if I'm gonna be able to take listenin' to this kinda music every day, but I'll try."

Kevin glanced back at his little brother Jordan moving the blocks and pointing at the letters. He whispered back, "I'm gonna try too. 'Cause I think the music's a good thing . . . a real good thing."

Chapter (8)

"ART SMART"

NOT WANTING TO GET OFF on the wrong foot, Kevin and Curtis were glad they had arrived on time for that first day of detention. They did, however, have a little trouble understanding how, in spite of all their effort, Melanie still managed to get to Mrs. Blake's room before them.

Anyone who'd spent time with Melanie knew she wasn't one to let anything get in her way when it came to visiting Mrs. Blake after school. And the boys figured it must have been her excitement about visiting her favorite teacher that gave her extra fuel. And that extra fuel gave her the power to make it there before anyone else.

On this day, Kevin and Curtis were just glad and grateful they had been able to make it on time. However, once inside, they had to come face-to-face with a very important fact. For the next two weeks they would be sharing space with Melanie—whether they liked it or not.

At Mrs. Blake's direction, they started in cautiously, with neither boy knowing what to expect. They wondered whether they'd have to define yet another enormous vocabulary assignment. This time, maybe it would be a list of one hundred words or more—to keep them extremely busy for the two weeks. That would certainly be intimidating enough to make Mr. Dunn's assignment look like nothing.

Curtis, who was ready to admit that math was his hardest subject, also feared they might receive an equal number of math problems. But when he remembered the deal he'd made with Kevin to do whatever they were given, he resolved that no matter how hard he had to struggle to complete two week's worth of math problems, he would do it.

Since they understood why they were there, Kevin and Curtis were bewildered by Mrs. Blake's warm welcome. She motioned with her hand again for them to come all the way into the room.

"Come right in," she said sweetly.

Curtis nudged Kevin in the arm. "That means she's comin' in for the kill."

"Whadaya mean?" Kevin whispered.

"You'll see. Ain't nobody that nice . . . nobody."

By now Melanie had moved on to straightening up the books on the bookshelf. Kevin could see Jordan sitting alone at the small round table. Placed directly in front of him were a large sheet of white paper and a box of crayons. With his back facing Kevin, Jordan was unaware that his brother had entered the room.

Mrs. Blake pointed to the far right side of the room. "Kevin, you and Curtis take a seat at that table over there."

Without question they immediately did as they were told. They put their book bags next to two chairs and sat down.

"I'll be right back," she told them.

They tried to appear calm, but Kevin sat rubbing his hands together while Curtis's lower lip trembled; his eyes followed Mrs. Blake's every step right to her desk. The gentle music continued playing and as hard as the two boys tried to ignore the beautiful melodies, they couldn't help but recognize how all the instruments neatly fit together in perfect harmonies that cushioned the sweet melody above it.

The frown that had been forming earlier on Curtis's face had now fully formed, but Kevin found himself liking the strange music. It was relaxing and, just like Mrs. Blake's room, it made him feel warm and good all over.

And more than that, when he glanced over at the table where his brother sat, he watched Jordan as he picked up a crayon and began to move it slowly across the smooth white drawing paper. This was something new and Kevin wondered if maybe the music had something to do with Jordan's new desire to add color to the blank page.

As the music played, Kevin soon witnessed Jordan's little hand grasping onto another color and blending it into his creation. Since he was too far away to see, Kevin used his imagination to give form to the little boy's picture. It took a whole lot of self-control to keep from bolting out of his seat and running over to congratulate Jordan. More than anything he wanted to tell him how beautiful his picture was. But to leave his seat without permission would be a mistake.

So from a distance, Kevin silently celebrated what he saw as another milestone in Jordan's life. And he was glad about what he considered a small miracle. He remembered that first time when he had come to Mrs. Blake's class with Melanie and saw the kind teacher praying. He had thought it strange and unusual. But now, as he sat gazing at his brother moving his hand back and forth across what otherwise would have remained a mere blank sheet of paper, he wondered if her prayer had been for Jordan.

For that moment, Kevin set aside the guilty feelings he was having about getting into trouble at his new school and at home. He allowed himself a moment to rejoice in knowing that his little brother had come to a classroom with colorful bright walls and pictures.

How wonderful for him to have a teacher who spoke to him softly and who welcomed and accepted him. Jordan had been blessed to be part of a classroom where the teacher played pretty music for him. And maybe the only way he knew how to say thank you was in coloring something beautiful on his paper.

Kevin found himself beginning to understand why Melanie wanted to be there. Mrs. Blake's room was very special; it was more special than any other classroom Kevin had ever entered before. And though he and Curtis were there because they'd been assigned detention, Kevin was starting to feel like maybe this was the best possible place they could be.

"I have something for you two. Please come here."

The sound of Mrs. Blake's voice summoned Kevin back to reality. He figured it was time to receive his assignment; most likely it was an assignment that would probably take the entire two weeks to complete. Suddenly Kevin saw Mr. Dunn's word list flash before his eyes and in his head he began multiplying that list times ten. He accepted the fact that he and Curtis deserved whatever punishment awaited them at Mrs. Blake's desk, but he hoped for leniency nonetheless.

Curtis looked at Kevin and Kevin looked at Curtis. Both of them knew they were about to meet their fate. Kevin decided to be the courageous one and stepped out in front and walked up to Mrs. Blake's desk. Curtis trailed a few steps behind, but when he reached the front of the room, he stood right next to Kevin. And though she hadn't been called, Melanie also went to Mrs. Blake's desk too while Jordan continued coloring.

Mrs. Blake picked up a poster from her desk. "I understand you two boys like to draw big pictures. Am I right?"

Kevin wasn't sure how he should answer her question. He glanced over at Curtis and could tell his friend had already decided to remain silent. Kevin knew that she was waiting for a response, but he was afraid if he gave the wrong answer, it might result in his getting into more trouble.

Like Curtis, he convinced himself that the safest thing would probably be to say nothing. However, when he thought about it a little more, he reminded himself that Mrs. Blake was already fully aware of what they had done. So Kevin figured, in this case, answering the question truthfully couldn't hurt.

"Yes, I like to draw," Kevin said politely.

"Me too," Curtis added cautiously.

"Good, then this will be the right assignment for you to work on when you come after school." Mrs. Blake held up a paper that announced a school district–wide poster contest. "I think anyone as interested in art as I hear you boys are should want to enter this."

Kevin looked excited, while Curtis looked skeptical. "You mean, for detention you're gonna let us draw?" Curtis asked.

"Yes, but this is an extremely important assignment. If it's not taken seriously, then we'll have to find a more suitable punishment." Mrs. Blake reached for another paper that she had neatly folded and placed in her top desk drawer. "Here it is," she said as she opened it up. "This year's theme is 'Kids Helping Kids Build Good Character.'" She continued, "It's a contest for students who attend schools in the city of Philadelphia. And the poster chosen for first place here at Harriet Tubman will receive a prize of $150 and a blue ribbon." Mrs. Blake looked directly at the two boys. "You don't have to enter the contest if you don't want to, but I'd like to see you give your best effort toward completing the project."

"I wanna help!" Melanie shouted.

Curtis put up his hand to let Melanie know he was against her participating. "No, you just want part of our money 'cause you think we're gonna win."

Hoping to convince Kevin and Curtis to let her take part, Melanie gave it another try. "No I don't. You might not even enter the contest, but I still wanna help."

Melanie was surprised when Kevin came to her defense. "But she does have good ideas and she's smart," Kevin added.

Right away he could see that Curtis didn't take kindly to his remark. "You don't think we're smart?" Curtis charged.

"The way I see it, with her brain workin' on our side, it can only help us win."

Although still reluctant to have Melanie on board, Curtis agreed. "If we do win, she's not getting as much as we get."

Melanie folded her arms tightly and spoke firmly. "And why is that, Curtis Givens?"

"'Cause me and Kevin'll be doing all the hard stuff."

". . . hard stuff like what?" she countered.

"We'll be doin' the drawing," Curtis replied.

Melanie unfolded her arms and raised her right hand to let Curtis know she was about to make an important point. "I can draw too, ya know. Last year I even got a blue ribbon on the African picture I drew for the school cultural art show . . . remember, Mrs. Blake?"

"Yes, Melanie, it was a beautiful drawing."

It was obvious that Curtis wasn't swayed one bit by the support Melanie had gotten from Mrs. Blake. It was also clear that he wasn't going to win his argument to keep Melanie off the project either.

"All right!" he said, throwing his hands up in disgust. "You can draw! Just don't get in our way! Right, Kevin?"

Kevin hesitated for a few seconds then said, "C'mon, let's see if we can come up with an idea."

"How long do we have to get the poster done, Mrs. Blake?" Melanie asked.

Mrs. Blake checked the bottom portion of the paper she held in her hand. "It says it must be completed by February 21 so it can be judged by March 15."

Curtis appeared concerned. He began counting on his fingers and then suddenly stopped. "That only gives us two weeks!"

Kevin wasn't sure about the amount of time either, but he tried to seem confident. "Don't worry, we'll get it done."

For the remainder of the time left for that day, Curtis and

Kevin, along with Melanie, took a seat at the back table and discussed their ideas. Melanie wrote down everything that was said. Curtis wanted a picture of students holding hands. Kevin wanted to draw a scene showing students reaching their hands high into the air. Then Melanie suggested a drawing with children of different races helping one another in different ways.

"I don't get it." Curtis was quick to question her on it.

Kevin agreed. "Me neither."

Melanie knew if her idea had any chance of being chosen for the project, she had to get Curtis and Kevin to understand it. "It's like the way that I help Jordan with the blocks. I take my time and I feel good when he does what I do. That's what we need to show in the poster—kids helping other kids."

She could see by the expressions on the boys' faces that they finally understood her idea.

"I think it's good," Kevin said. His voice sounded relieved, knowing they had accomplished something good on their first day. "Whataya think, Curtis?"

Curtis knew it was a good idea but didn't want to give any credit to Melanie for having thought of it.

"I guess it's all right, if we can't come up with nothing else."

Melanie sensed that Curtis liked the idea too, but he wasn't going to give her the satisfaction of hearing him say so. She didn't complain because she knew that was as good as she was going to get in the way of a vote of confidence from Curtis.

"So," she said, "we'll meet tomorrow and start drawing. Okay?"

Curtis wasn't happy because it looked as though, in an instant, Melanie had put herself in charge of the project.

"Yeah, whatever," he said, picking up his book bag. "See ya, Kevin."

Kevin waved good-bye. "See ya," he said. He walked over to where Jordan was sitting and began picking up the crayons and putting them back in the box. Suddenly, Jordan let out that excruciating scream. Kevin covered his ears and Melanie immediately interceded.

"Wait!" she yelled. "Watch what I do." She picked up a crayon and placed it in the box. She then picked up another one and handed it to Jordan so he could put it in the box. She did that until all the crayons were off the table and back in the box.

His smile revealed how pleased he was that his little brother had learned to put his crayons away. It was a simple task, yet Kevin knew that he had just witnessed something very special.

Kevin thought maybe things were starting to take a turn for the better. He also realized that his friendship with Melanie was very much "on" again. Working with Curtis and Melanie would bring together the best of both worlds. Everyone at Harriet Tubman Elementary knew that Melanie was "book smart." She could read and write very well and had all kinds of awards to prove it. However, Curtis Givens and Kevin Manning were "art smart" and dared anyone to challenge that fact.

Kevin then thought about the amount of smarts that existed between them and could see only one word describing their group—*WINNERS!*

TWO PLUS TWO

THE NEXT DAY Melanie wanted Kevin and Curtis to see her as a valuable member of the group, so she pretended that she wasn't the least bit interested in what they were working on. She wondered if the boys had already forgotten they'd told her she could help. Unfortunately, her holding out only lasted about fifteen minutes. After stretching her neck as far as she could to try and get a peek, she finally gave up and walked over to them.

"How come you're so quiet back here?" she asked. This was the best way she could think of to start a conversation. She leaned over and visually studied the outline Kevin and Curtis had drawn on paper.

"What's it supposed to be?"

Curtis didn't turn around to answer her. He kept on working. Kevin, on the other hand, did stop and look up at her. He enjoyed the fact that Melanie was so curious.

"It's gonna be a poster," he said proudly. "And when we're done, we're gonna enter it in that contest Mrs. Blake was talkin' about. And it's gonna win!"

The excitement Kevin felt must have been contagious because Melanie instantly wanted to hear more, especially after their conversation yesterday. She assumed she'd be included in every stage of the project. So it was surprising to find that she had been excluded from the great plans being made.

"I can see it's a poster, but didn't you say that I could work on it too?"

Suddenly, Curtis spoke up. "We'll let you know when we need you to do something."

"But I wanna work on it from the beginning," she said firmly.

Curtis turned to face Kevin and away from Melanie. "*We're* gonna enter it in the school district-wide contest, right Kevin? And, *we're* gonna win the $150. I can feel it!"

Just for a second, Curtis turned his head to get a glimpse of Melanie's reaction. He could tell his words were stinging to her ears but offered no excuse for what he said or the way that he said it. He shook his head as though telling her she was wasting her time and then resumed his drawing. He couldn't understand why Kevin bothered telling Melanie, of all people, about their plans anyway. "Gotta finish it before the deadline," Curtis said.

Kevin figured it was Curtis's way of telling him it was time to get back to work. Kevin could tell Melanie was very interested, but didn't say another word. Like Curtis, he resumed his drawing. Melanie was left standing over them and just had to accept the fact that their conversation was over. She turned to go back to the table with Jordan when suddenly she couldn't hold it in any longer. The power of wanting to be a part of the project overtook any prideful feelings she may have had. It caused Melanie to offer her assistance once again.

"C'mon, let me help," she pleaded. "You're gonna need somebody to do the coloring when you're done with the drawing, right?"

"No girls!" Curtis snapped. "We got this."

Melanie knew Curtis had a vote, but surely his wasn't the last word. Kevin had a right to say something too about who could and couldn't help.

"Kevin, can I help?" she pleaded. "I'll work hard and I'll color real neat. Just give me a chance. I won't mess anything up."

Kevin could feel the weight of the pressure coming from these two and it made him feel like a wishbone about to be broken. Both Melanie and Curtis had their attention on Kevin, wondering what his answer would be.

Curtis stopped drawing. He didn't want to miss any part of hearing Kevin say no. *Finally*, he told himself, *Kevin will put Melanie in her place and maybe she'll leave us alone.* Curtis looked pretty confident about what Kevin's answer was going to be. He gave Melanie the same look that Alex Martinez always gave him. The look that said "loser" and echoed the words, "there's no place for you here." It was coming and probably sat right on the tip of Kevin's tongue.

He placed his pencil on the floor, sat upright, and folded his hands. "Go on, Kevin," he encouraged his friend, " . . . tell her to git lost."

Curtis didn't understand, but Kevin could see it in Melanie's eyes. Right now, helping out on the poster was the most important thing in the world to her. He didn't want to choose, but he knew he had to. Picking up an extra pencil, he handed it to her. "Can ya draw?"

Melanie gave him that look of confidence she was known for around the school. "Of course, I can," she said with her hand shaking just a bit. "But I think I'd really rather color."

There was no question about it. Curtis was more than highly dissatisfied with Kevin's answer. He was livid. He got up off the floor and threw down his pencil. "Well, if she's workin' on this thing, I ain't!"

Mrs. Blake had been sitting at her desk correcting papers, all the while listening and hoping the three children would resolve their differences. And until now, she refrained from interfering. She wanted Melanie, Kevin, and Curtis to come up with a solution that all three of them could live with.

Melanie was just about to give up when she remembered something she'd heard Mrs. Blake say about the theme for the contest. "You're drawing something about kids helping kids, right?"

Curtis was determined not to give Melanie even a foothold of a chance to work on the project. "Yeah, so what? That don't mean we got to let you get in our way."

"I just think it's kinda hard to make a real good poster; I mean, a winning poster about working together when you're having so much trouble workin' with *other people*."

Kevin could see Melanie's point. "She's right, you know. It'll probably turn out a whole lot better if we put *all* of our best ideas down. C'mon, Curtis, let's try. You wanna win, right?"

Though he refused to admit it, Curtis knew Kevin was right.

Besides, he couldn't deny that they had already sort of agreed the day before that she could work with them.

"Well, if she's gonna be workin' on this, then she's gotta be on your side and stay outta my way."

That was Curtis's compromise so Melanie and Kevin knew if she was going to join them, they'd have to accept his terms.

"Don't worry," Melanie said. "I'll stay out of your way."

"Ugh," Curtis grumbled as he picked up his pencil and went back to work.

While their solution wasn't all of what she'd hoped for, Mrs. Blake was pleased to see that the children had worked out their differences on their own. It certainly hadn't ended as smoothly as it could have, but it did result in an understanding between them.

When she stepped over to get a look at what they were doing, it made her glad to see how involved they were in putting their ideas on paper. In fact, they were so intent about making progress that they didn't even see Mrs. Blake standing there. More importantly, they also didn't realize it was time to go home.

Finally, Melanie turned around and noticed Mrs. Blake standing behind them pointing at the clock. She winked at Melanie, letting her know she had done well and succeeded in negotiating.

Mrs. Blake cleared her throat. "Ahem!"

Kevin and Curtis stopped drawing and turned around. "It's time to go home, boys," she said. "You're finished for today."

"Can I just do this part?" Curtis pleaded while positioning his pencil to continue drawing. No one would have ever thought or believed they'd see Curtis Givens begging to stay in detention once it was officially over. It was pretty clear he had forgotten that detention was the reason why he was there.

Truly, he had never enjoyed himself so much staying after school as he did that afternoon. And now, Curtis Givens, just like the others, had begun feeling the special flavor and welcoming atmosphere that drew Melanie back to Mrs. Blake's room time and time again.

"I'm sorry," she said. "It's getting late. The good news is you can all come back tomorrow and work on your project some more."

Curtis didn't want to leave, but he understood that it was time to go home. He lifted the poster up high for Mrs. Blake to see.

"Whataya think? You like it, Mrs. Blake?"

Mrs. Blake was savvy enough to know that she wouldn't be able to fool Curtis if she didn't like what they'd drawn. She reached for the poster board and held it in her hands. What they had managed to finish had been drawn in pencil, so it was difficult for her to see it clearly against the blue background of the poster board. Mrs. Blake took her finger and traced around the outline of the picture.

When Curtis, Kevin, and Melanie saw the smile on her face, they knew she liked what she saw.

"It's really good," she told them. "I like it."

It was easy to see that getting Mrs. Blake's seal of approval made all the difference in the world, and it was the perfect way to end the afternoon.

"Think we'll win, Mrs. Blake?" Melanie asked.

"Whattaya mean *we*?" Curtis scowled.

Melanie was quick to pull herself out of the question. "Sorry, I mean them."

Surprisingly, Kevin came to her defense. "If we all do the work, then we *all* share if we win. Right, Curtis?"

Curtis still wasn't 100 percent in favor of Melanie working with them on the project, but knew what he had to do in order to keep the peace. "Ah, whatever . . . okay."

Kevin smiled. He didn't want to spend any more time this day trying to convince Curtis that Melanie was an equal part of their team. He walked over to help Jordan put away his crayons and paper, while Mrs. Blake turned off the classical music that had soothed the children's ears for the afternoon.

Suddenly, Kevin called out, "Hey, c'mere!"

Everyone hurried to the back table to see what Kevin was so excited about.

"Wow!" said Curtis. "Look at that!"

Mrs. Blake gently picked up Jordan's paper and studied it in amazement. Melanie placed her hand on Jordan's shoulder and whispered in his ear, "It's beautiful!"

The four of them stood around the peculiar little boy who rarely spoke or smiled and were astonished at the extraordinary coloring he had done on his paper. Every color had been perfectly shaded within the lines of his picture. Melanie was right. For the first time in his life, Jordan had created something so wonderful that if they hadn't been in the room the whole time, they wouldn't have believed what they saw.

Kevin helped his little brother into his coat while Mrs. Blake took the picture and hung it at the very top of her "Good Work" bulletin board.

"Look, Jordan!" Kevin said, pointing at the drawing. "You did that, Jordan! You did that!"

"He can help us with the poster too!" Melanie exclaimed. "We can do the coloring—me and Jordan together!"

Curtis knew he'd been outvoted on everything else, so there was no point in trying to protest letting Jordan help with the poster. Besides, he could see how wonderful the little boy's coloring was. He knew right away, Jordan would be a true asset to their group. Kevin looked over at Curtis to find out where he stood on Melanie's suggestion.

"If he colors the poster the way he did that picture, we're really gonna win."

"That's it then," Melanie declared. "It's two plus two. You two can draw and we can do the coloring!"

After putting on his jacket, Curtis loaded on his backpack and only offered a half grin.

Kevin, on the other hand, clearly liked the idea. While he helped Jordan with his jacket, Kevin couldn't help but be pleased with what was happening. *This will be the first time*, he thought, *that me and Jordan will work on something together*. And he looked forward to it.

"Yeah," Kevin said. "Sounds like 'two plus two' to me. C'mon, Jordan," he said as he took his brother by the hand and grabbed his lunch box off the shelf. "See ya, Mrs. Blake," Kevin called out as they made their way out of the room. "We gotta lot to talk about on the way home, Jordan . . . a whole lot."

Chapter 10

MASTERPIECE!

TWO WEEKS DETENTION had gone by faster than either Kevin or Curtis believed was possible. Maybe it was because the past ten days they'd spent in Mrs. Blake's room never really seemed like detention at all. Neither of the boys had expressed to the other how he felt, but it was interesting how their thoughts about leaving were identical.

Inwardly, they had to admit, when faced with the reality that their required daily reporting time was over, they found themselves surprised that neither of them wanted it to end. For the past ten days they had been able to do something they truly loved. And they were overjoyed about the way their poster had turned out.

Though putting their feelings into words was difficult, they sensed nothing but joy moving through every muscle and bone in their bodies. It was unexplainable, but somehow during those afternoon sessions, they too had allowed themselves to become embraced by the marvelous feeling that characterized Mrs. Blake's classroom. Alive and rich with color, it was warming to the heart and inspiring to their souls.

Also, during this time, something else wonderful had happened. Kevin and Curtis found themselves liking those classical selections by Mozart that Mrs. Blake always played during their afternoons together. The music brought to life the beautiful pictures and posters and everything else that seemed to tell the unique story that was characteristic of Mrs. Blake's room. They would have never admitted it at the beginning, but the music added to helping her room feel like the most comfortable place on earth.

Then there was something else everyone learned during this time. Kevin and Curtis weren't the only ones who had come to appreciate Mrs. Blake's interesting musical selections. Jordan liked them too. Once he was settled into his chair and given a picture, he'd color with the preciseness of a professional. No one could explain what was happening, but everyone agreed that the combination of colors he used in his pictures was astounding.

Truly, Jordan had an unusual gift that had somehow been awakened when the music started. The same little boy who said only a few words, and seldom smiled, was now bringing smiles to others by the care and brilliancy shown in his work. Watching Jordan color made Kevin proud and pleased that he had been introduced to a part of his little brother that, until the music began, he never knew existed.

Kevin, Curtis, and Melanie decided not to show Mrs. Blake the poster again until it was completely finished. And Mrs. Blake, not wanting to take away from their excitement in any way, agreed not to peek until it was all done. Each day when they stopped working, one of them would take the poster to the back of the room and place it in the supply closet, making sure the picture was facing the wall.

But today was Friday, and if they planned to enter the contest, they had to make their decision because the judging would take place on the following Monday. It was time to reveal to Mrs. Blake the scene that the group had worked so enthusiastically to finish for the past two weeks. The very last detail was to have each of them sign their names on the back of the poster. To the sound of everyone's applause, Jordan, who had learned to write the letter "J," wrote the beginning letter of his first name on the back of the poster when Melanie placed a pencil in his hand.

Melanie went to get Mrs. Blake. She grabbed her hand and urged her to come to the back of the room where the others were waiting.

"Don't look! Okay, Mrs. Blake?"

"I won't," she said, covering her eyes with one of her hands. She allowed Melanie to carefully guide her to the back of the room. The minute Melanie's footsteps stopped, so did hers.

"Ya ready, Mrs. Blake?" Curtis asked.

"Yes, I'm ready."

"Ya sure?" asked Kevin.

"I'm sure."

"We're gonna count to three," said Melanie, "then you can look."

Kevin helped Jordan and made sure he got a spot right next to him. All at once Melanie, Kevin, and Curtis started their count: "One . . . two . . . three!"

When Mrs. Blake removed her hand from her face, she beheld

what she really believed could be the winning poster in the contest. At first, she didn't say a word. Instead, she gestured for the children to bring it closer. And as she beheld the scene depicted, she stood silently shaking her head.

Melanie walked over and softly touched her arm. "Do you like it, Mrs. Blake?"

Curtis thought he saw a tear roll down the left side of Mrs. Blake's cheek. "Yes, I do. I think it's wonderful."

"Wonderful enough to win?" Kevin asked.

"Wonderful enough to be a masterpiece," she answered.

Kevin could tell Mrs. Blake's response was a good one, but he wasn't exactly sure how good. He wanted to hear more. "What's a masterpiece?"

Melanie didn't give Mrs. Blake a chance to reply. She saw this as an opportunity to show off her smarts and blurted out the answer. "It means our poster shows our work was done with great skill. It's extraordinary! Right, Mrs. Blake?"

Mrs. Blake was still admiring the poster that she now held in her hands. Shaking her head, she smiled. "Yes, Melanie, I would definitely say it's extraordinary."

Curtis was pleased but didn't say anything. When he looked to his right, he thought he saw something even more extraordinary than their picture. He thought he saw Jordan smile. And that made him smile all the way from the inside out.

Although he would be the last one on earth to say it, Curtis was starting to believe what Melanie was always telling everyone about Mrs. Blake being the best teacher in the world. And as he stood before her wearing the proudest grin he could muster, he believed she might very well be the smartest teacher in the world as well.

Chapter (11)

THE ENTRY

AS FAR AS CURTIS was concerned, there was nothing more to say. Mrs. Blake had given their poster the highest rating imaginable. She had called it a "masterpiece." The time had come to enter it in the contest.

"Where do we take it? Who do we give it to?" Melanie asked eagerly.

Mrs. Blake walked back to the front of the room and took down the information about the contest she'd posted on the bulletin board behind her desk. "Here it is," she said, handing the paper to Curtis. "Look it over carefully to be sure you've followed all the rules."

Curtis passed the paper to Melanie knowing she would check the requirements thoroughly. They quickly returned to the back of the room and confirmed their poster size and examined the scene they'd created once again making sure it was based on the given theme. Suddenly Curtis saw a change in Melanie's eyes and knew something was very wrong. Curious to find out what caused the change in her expression, he immediately wanted an answer. "What's the matter?"

Kevin could tell something was different too. "Yeah, what is it?"

Melanie pointed at one detail that now became very important. It had been written in small print at the very bottom of the paper, and Mrs. Blake had missed it. "Jordan's too little to be in the contest," she said regretfully.

Kevin made it no secret that he disagreed with the rule. "Whaddaya talking about?"

Melanie signaled for Kevin and Curtis to come closer. "Look right here," she said putting her finger next to the tiny letters. "This says only kids in grades four to sixth can participate."

"So what are we gonna do?" Kevin asked. "Does this mean we can't be in the contest?"

"We can ask Mrs. Blake," Melanie suggested.

Curtis intentionally spoke in a hushed voice. "No," he protested. "She'll say we can't be in it and I did all this work for nothing." Taking the same pencil Jordan had used to write the letter "J" Curtis turned the poster over and erased it. "It we take Jordan's name off and turn it in, we'll give him his part of the prize when we win."

Kevin could tell by the look on Melanie's face that she thought Curtis's idea was a bad one. When he glanced over at Jordan he felt troubled knowing his little brother would get no credit for the work he did. "But if Jordan's name is not on the poster, it's like he didn't do any of it."

Curtis was quick to give a reminder. "But if his name is on it, then none of us will get credit because we can't be in the contest."

Kevin was convinced that Curtis was right about leaving Jordan's name off of the poster. Melanie didn't agree, but chose to remain silent. Kevin tapped her lightly on the arm. "At least *we'll* know how much Jordan helped."

"Yeah . . . we'll know," Melanie said sadly.

The four of them walked back to Mrs. Blake's desk. "Everything looks good," Curtis announced.

"Then you can take your entry to Mr. Snead in the guidance office," she told them. "He'll register it for the contest."

Kevin and Melanie looked at the clock. It was almost 3:20 p.m. and soon everyone would be gone for the day.

"Can we go, Mrs. Blake?" Kevin pleaded. "It's Friday, and we don't want Mr. Snead to leave before we can give him our poster."

"Remember," Melanie added. "The judging is on Monday."

"Yeah," said Curtis. "The worse thing that could happen is we did all this work for nothing because we didn't turn it in on time."

Mrs. Blake could feel the anxiousness in the room about to boil over. "Yes, go ahead and take it to the guidance office." Then right away she put up her finger signaling for them to wait. "Here," she said quickly scribbling a note. "Give this to Mr. Snead along with your poster."

Melanie smiled because she knew Mrs. Blake wasn't taking any chances. Just in case Mr. Snead said they were too late, she gave them a note explaining that she was responsible for the delay.

"Thank you, Mrs. Blake," Melanie said politely.

"Yeah, thanks!" Curtis echoed.

Kevin reached into his pocket and pulled out a note of his own. "Thank you, Mrs. Blake." Handing her the folded piece of paper, he watched her eyes glisten as she read it.

When she finished, she smiled at Kevin, letting him know that she was pleased about what the note revealed. "I knew you could do it," she said.

"I didn't forget," he told her.

"I know you didn't," Mrs. Blake assured him.

"Do what?" interrupted Melanie. "What'd Kevin do?"

"Never you mind, young lady," Mrs. Blake was quick to say. "Everything's fine."

Kevin was about to take Jordan by the hand when Mrs. Blake leaned down and looked into his eyes. "And I'm so very proud of you too, Jordan," she said.

Curtis was carefully holding the poster like it was a priceless work of art. He and the others were headed out the door when he handed it to Melanie and raced back inside the classroom.

"Yes Curtis?" Mrs. Blake asked.

Without uttering a word, he reached down into his pocket and brought out a crumpled piece of paper of his own and handed to her. The enormous grin on his face revealed that whatever message was written on the paper, he was proud about it.

"Go ahead, Mrs. Blake," he urged. "Read it."

Once again, Mrs. Blake read the contents of the note and couldn't restrain the joy Curtis could see in her eyes.

"And I knew you could do it too, Curtis Givens."

The smile on Mrs. Blake's face had bounced its way onto Curtis's. "Thank you, Mrs. Blake."

It had taken a while, but in that one afternoon, Mrs. Blake held in her hands the note from Mr. Rayner that Kevin had promised to give her after receiving that first detention. The note informed her that Kevin was doing good work and stated that Mr. Rayner was greatly pleased with his behavior in class.

Mrs. Blake was even happier that the note Curtis brought her said the same. His grades and his behavior in Mr. Rayner's class had improved. Curtis was happy about his progress and wanted to share the news with her. The really wonderful part was in knowing she had never asked Curtis for a note, but he had begun to care enough that he wanted her to have it.

Mrs. Blake didn't want Curtis to miss the others, but could tell he had something else on his mind. He stood quietly before her as though he believed she could read his thoughts.

"Is there something else, Curtis?"

"Yes," he said softly. "Would you . . . say a prayer for us? . . . that we could win the contest?"

Mrs. Blake realized that the most important lesson Curtis had learned during the time he'd spent in her room extended far beyond the artwork.

"I would be happy to ask the Lord to bless the work you all did, but it won't guarantee you're going to win."

"I know," he said, heading toward the door. "I just think it'll give us a better chance."

Before anything else could be said, Curtis left and was on his way to catch up with the others. Melanie turned around and saw Curtis running to catch up. "Hurry up!" she yelled.

"C'mon, Jordan," Kevin said, proudly taking his brother by the hand. "We're gonna turn in our poster! Try n' walk faster."

When they got to Mr. Snead's office, his door was open wide enough for them to see him sitting at his desk and reading a newspaper. He was holding a cup in his hand and leaning over his desk. Every few seconds or so, he would carefully sip from his cup and return his attention to the paper. Whatever he was reading must have been funny because when the children saw him laugh, they took that as their cue to knock on the door and go in.

Curtis was in front, but Melanie put up her hand and he stopped.

"Better let me go first," she insisted.

Kevin could tell by the annoyed look on Curtis's face that he wasn't at all pleased with Melanie's suggestion.

"I don't see why you hafta go in first," he said. Pointing at Kevin, he went on, "Plus, we did way more work on this than *you* did."

"That's not why I said that," Melanie told him. "I said it because the only time you go to see Mr. Snead is when you're in trouble for something. And from what I've heard he's seen you a whole lot lately. I just don't want him to get the wrong idea before we get the chance to give him the poster."

"She's got a point," Kevin reluctantly agreed. "Maybe we oughta let Melanie go first."

Curtis realized Melanie's reason for wanting to step out front was understandable, so he stepped back and let her walk past him.

"Go on, Melanie," he told her.

Kevin held on to Jordan and the three of them marched into Mr. Snead's office directly behind Melanie.

"Hi, Mr. Snead!" she announced cheerfully.

Obviously startled, he jumped a bit. Luckily, though, he didn't spill any of the hot liquid from his cup. He closed his paper and removed his glasses. However, the children could see they had disturbed him. He quickly shoved his newspaper aside and set down his cup.

Peering past Curtis, Kevin could see Mr. Snead had been reading the comic strip page in the newspaper. He wanted to ask him which ones were his favorites but decided it wasn't the right time.

"What can I do for you, Melanie?" Looking around her, Mr. Snead focused his attention on the three boys standing behind her.

She reached back to get the poster from Curtis. "We want to submit our poster for the contest. The judging's gonna be on Monday, right?"

Mr. Snead was taken aback at seeing Curtis. "Curtis? You're entering the contest?"

Stepping right up next to Melanie, Curtis proudly said, "Yep!"

Mr. Snead was surprised by Curtis's response and asked further, "You mean, the 'Kids Helping Kids' poster contest?"

Seeing Mr. Snead's disbelief made Curtis realize Melanie had been right. The only times he'd ever spoken to Mr. Snead was when he had done something wrong. And it was clear, Mr. Snead was having difficulty seeing Curtis any other way.

Melanie was just about to hand the poster to Mr. Snead, when he pointed at the clock on the wall. "You know," he said, "the deadline was 3:00 p.m. *sharp*. It's now twenty-five minutes after."

"I knew it!" Curtis snapped angrily.

"Shush!" Kevin warned. "Melanie, give Mr. Snead the note."

"Oh yeah," she announced, pulling out the note as though

it were an official document. "Mrs. Blake gave me this note to give you."

Mr. Snead hurriedly read the note. "Hmmm . . . ," he grumbled. "Where's your entry?"

Melanie was relieved to finally place the valuable poster into Mr. Snead's hands. From the moment she let go of it, all eyes were on Mr. Snead. They watched him as he studied the scene they'd created for their poster. And when they saw the tremendous smile come upon his face, they immediately knew everything was all right.

"You like it?" Kevin cautiously asked. He pulled his little brother closer to him.

"It's amazing . . . absolutely amazing," Mr. Snead told them. For more than a few minutes, he glanced at the poster and then at the children. Then he'd look at the poster again. Once again, he repeated the word softly, "amazing."

"So, can we be in the contest?" Melanie asked boldly.

"Yes, your poster will definitely be in the contest. The judging will take place on Monday, you know. And the winning entry will be announced sometime that same day."

Kevin moved closer to Mr. Snead's desk. "Think we gotta a chance at winnin'?"

"I'm not one of the judges. But I can tell you, this is one of the best posters I've seen. I think you've got better than a good chance at winning that contest."

"Yes!" Kevin exclaimed. "You hear that, Curtis? Even Mr. Snead thinks we got a good chance of winnin'!"

"And who might this little fella be?" Mr. Snead asked, pointing at Jordan.

"He's my little brother, Jordan," Kevin said.

"Nice to meet you Jordan," Mr. Snead said heartily.

"You like it Mr. Snead? I helped too," Melanie boasted.

"Yeah, she helped a lot," Curtis said.

Melanie rightfully looked surprised. That was the first time Curtis had ever given her credit for anything. "Thanks, Curtis."

Curtis merely threw back his hand and pretended to stare at the poster.

Meanwhile, Jordan slid his little hand back and forth across the smooth edge of Mr. Snead's desk.

"This truly is remarkable," said Mr. Snead. "You really did miss the deadline you know. But since you have this note from Mrs. Blake, I'm sure there won't be a problem."

Melanie became very excited. "Are you gonna be there, Mr. Snead?"

"Yes, I wouldn't miss this year's contest for anything in the world."

"Why?" asked Kevin.

"Because," said Mr. Snead as he held the poster up high above their heads, "I believe I'm looking at the winner."

Kevin, Curtis, and Melanie left Mr. Snead's office that Friday afternoon feeling as though their poster had already been named the grand prize winner. As far as they were concerned, holding the contest was merely a formality. As they happily walked down the corridor, the only thing keeping their feet on the ground was the law of gravity. Even little Jordan appeared to have a newfound gladness in his step while trying to keep up the pace set by the others.

When they reached the top of the ramp, Curtis stopped. "I

forgot something," he said. "Wait for me, I'll be right back."

He hurried to Mr. Snead's office hoping he hadn't left for the day. When he peeked inside, he was pleased to find him still reading his newspaper. "Excuse me Mr. Snead," he said knocking lightly on the door.

Mr. Snead waved for Curtis to come inside. "What can I do for you, Curtis?"

Curtis could see that Mr. Snead had placed their poster on top of a pile of other entries on a small table near the window. "I just need to check one more thing on our poster."

"Go ahead, but please be quick. I'll be leaving soon."

Curtis walked over to the table, looked back at Mr. Snead, and pretended to check the poster. In a few seconds he was on his way out the door. "Thanks Mr. Snead!"

Mr. Snead answered without lifting his eyes from his newspaper. "You're welcome Curtis."

Curtis was so glad to find his friends still waiting for him at the top of the ramp that suddenly he let out with a yell. "I can't wait until Monday!" Melanie looked at Kevin and Kevin looked at Melanie. They were surprised to hear that Curtis was looking forward to the next school day. They believed, if he could, he would skip right over the weekend and land squarely on Monday morning.

Melanie studied Curtis and wanted to ask him where he'd gone. However, she didn't want to ruin what had been a pretty good afternoon by prying.

Certainly there was no mystery concerning how good Curtis felt. And Melanie and Kevin believed they knew because they were experiencing the same joy. On Monday, all of the entries for the poster contest were going to be judged. It was clear that they were already seeing that blue ribbon being placed on their poster along with claiming the $150 prize money.

Besides knowing they had submitted a great entry, Curtis felt even more confident because he knew there was even more support on the way. Mrs. Blake had agreed to say a prayer for them and Curtis believed getting that extra help from heaven could only be to their advantage.

Chapter (12)

JUDGMENT DAY

CURTIS WAS SO EXCITED about the judging scheduled to take place that he set his alarm clock the night before so it would ring forty minutes earlier than usual the next morning. He wanted to make sure he was the very first student to arrive at school on Monday.

More amazing was the fact that, after having had such a hard time sleeping last night, he was able to rouse himself out of bed so easily. Every time he closed his eyes, all he could see was the big, blue, satiny ribbon being placed on their poster and the $150 prize money being placed in their hands.

Anyone who knew Curtis would understand that his showing up at school so early was truly something out of the ordinary. This was new for him, and his uncharacteristic arrival spoke of the importance he placed on the contest. For once, it was apparent that Curtis Givens had found something he deeply cared about. And that was enough to cause him to do things differently. The outcome of the contest was all he could think about. And he wanted to get inside that school building more than anything else in the world.

Some thought the genuine changes seen in Curtis came about because of his friendships with Kevin, Melanie, and little Jordan. Initially, picturing them all together was like trying to fit pieces into a puzzle when it was obvious the shapes and sizes were all wrong. But their friendship clearly ran deeper than what was visible from the outside. Somehow, the four of them working together on the poster had helped them appreciate the special talent each one possessed. And when they put those talents together, the fit was nothing short of perfection.

In her wisdom, Mrs. Blake had been able to see that perfection, even when the group of them couldn't. And while others may have readily given credit to the fact that good things were happening in Curtis's life because he'd finally found some friends, Curtis himself believed in his heart that God had heard Mrs. Blake's prayers. He truly suspected he had been favored with one of God's answers.

He hadn't told anyone, but he had prayed to have some friends, and now he felt good knowing he'd been blessed with some very special ones. So on this day very early in the morning, he had come to remind Mrs. Blake about a particular request he'd made.

Curtis watched and waited carefully as he saw teachers entering the main door of the school building. He was pretty sure Mrs. Blake had already arrived. Knowing he had to be very quiet, he took the first opportunity he got to enter the building unnoticed. He hurried up the corridor and around the corner to her classroom.

When he got there, he peeked through the window and saw her sitting at a table in the back of the room. Her head was bowed and her hands were folded. He knew that she was praying.

As gently as he could, he turned the doorknob and went inside. Curtis quietly tiptoed to the back of the room until he found himself standing next to Mrs. Blake. Although he tried not to disturb her, she heard him and lifted her head.

"Good morning, Curtis," she said cheerfully. "You're here pretty early today."

"Mornin', Mrs. Blake," he replied.

Curtis turned his head and looked away slightly, but his behavior convinced Mrs. Blake there was something on his mind. "So, what can I do for you on such a beautiful morning?"

"Today's the judging for the contest, ya know."

"Yes I know. Are you ready?"

Curtis waited. "Almost. I came to ask you somethin'."

"Yes, Curtis?"

"You remember what I asked you about on Friday?"

"You mean, when you asked me to pray about the contest?"

"Yeah. When I looked through your window, I saw you back here with your head down. Were you askin' God to help us win?"

Mrs. Blake looked at Curtis and could see in his eyes how much he wanted her to say yes.

"I did pray, Curtis, but I prayed for all of the students who entered the contest. And as I told you, a prayer is not a guarantee you're going to win. But it *is* a sure thing that God is listening. I can only pray that God's will be done and not my own. Sometimes what we want may not be what God wants for us. Do you understand?"

Curtis was disappointed but nodded to let Mrs. Blake know that he understood. However, he didn't fool her one bit. She could tell that he didn't. "God knows far better what each of us needs. We have to trust Him."

"Then He knows that I . . . I mean, *we* need to win that contest."

"What God chooses to give us may not be what we expect, but it is so much better than what we ask for, Curtis," Mrs. Blake explained.

Curtis nodded his head in agreement, but in his mind, he still hoped God would let them win. He surprised Mrs. Blake by giving her a quick hug and hurried out of the room. He told himself there couldn't possibly be anything better than being the winner of the contest.

"Thank you, Mrs. Blake!" he yelled on his way out into the hall.

"You're welcome, Curtis."

Curtis felt real good when he left Mrs. Blake's room. Something new was surely taking place in his life. Thinking about meeting up with Kevin, Melanie, and Jordan, he was starting to believe that God wasn't just hearing Mrs. Blake's prayers, He was also answering them.

Curtis was thinking about how much he liked working on the project with Kevin and Jordan. He even had to admit to himself, though he might be tempted to deny it if anyone asked, he really liked working with Melanie too. The new and improved

Curtis no longer went around writing on walls and had willingly given up the title "The Detention King." He didn't see himself that way anymore. He believed he was an artist and he knew he was a good one.

Waiting outside, he searched to see if any of the others had arrived. It was hard to think that Kevin, Melanie, and Jordan didn't see the urgency in getting to school early on such a great day. After all, in just a short time, they were going to be crowned winners of the school district-wide poster contest. Pretty soon, he could hear Kevin calling him.

"Curtis!" Kevin yelled as he came running up and pulling along little Jordan who was struggling to keep up. When he reached Curtis, Kevin took a deep breath and gave off a sigh of relief. "How long you been here?"

"I dunno," Curtis said. "But I been here a long time. When are they gonna ring the bell and let us in?" He stared at the huge doors of the main entrance as though expecting them to burst open at any second. Taking his eyes off the doors for just a moment, he nudged Kevin.

"You seen Melanie?"

"No, but I wouldn't worry 'bout her. She'll be here. Melanie wouldn't miss this day for nothing."

"Me neither!" Curtis laughed. "I been waitin' to get that smile off Alex's face ever since I came to this school. And today's the day!"

Just then Melanie walked up to where the three boys were standing. It only took one glance to notice how special this day was to her too. From head to toe, she had adorned herself in one of her beautiful Kente outfits. The three of them noticed how

Jordan couldn't seem to take his eyes off of the striking bright colors that made up Melanie's clothing. Her eyes were gleaming and her face was beaming with pride.

"Hey . . . everybody ready to win?"

"I know I am," Kevin answered in a most dignified way.

"I been ready since early this morning," Curtis bragged loudly.

"How early?" Melanie probed.

"Don't ask."

Within seconds of Curtis's comment, the school bell rang and a brand-new Monday was about to get underway.

"Finally!" he said, working his way inside and carving out a path so that he and Melanie could get through the crowd. This was a Monday that, if left to Curtis, would go down in history as the best one anybody had ever seen at Harriet Tubman Elementary School. He and Melanie were in the same homeroom, so as they veered off to the left on their way to class, Kevin darted in another direction, with Jordan fully in tow. They were heading toward the cafeteria. Kevin stopped and called out to Melanie and Curtis.

"You're not gonna eat breakfast?"

"I'm too nervous!" Melanie hollered back.

"Me too," said Curtis, while the two of them folded into the stream of students rushing to reach the sixth-grade hall.

"What time do ya think they'll have the judging?" Curtis asked Melanie.

"I dunno, but I hope it's as soon as we get to homeroom. I don't wanna have my stomach feelin' like this all day," she replied. "Plus, I'm feeling kinda bad about Jordan's name not being on the poster."

Curtis didn't want to tell Melanie, but his stomach was feeling kind of queasy too. He tried to keep his mind on the contest.

"Whatcha gonna do with your part of the prize money?" he inquired.

"I'm not sure. I wanna take some time and think about what I'm gonna do with it. It ain't a whole lot of money, ya know."

"I know, but I ain't never won nothin' before. Even if they wasn't givin' a prize, I just wanna know what it feels like to win," he explained.

Melanie had won lots of things. She was smart and everybody knew it. When it came to winning things, she and Curtis were exact opposites. She didn't know what it felt like to have never won anything, but she knew it must have felt pretty bad.

"We've got a good chance," she encouraged.

"No," said Curtis. "We got better than a good chance. Did you see the way Mrs. Blake looked at our poster? And, what about Mr. Snead? No, we're gonna win for sure. I can feel it all over."

Now Melanie could really see how important winning the contest was to Curtis. Working together with him had been more than just the four of them drawing and coloring for the last two weeks. For him, a very special door had been opened and Curtis Givens had allowed himself to walk through it. And when he did, what he found on the other side was the beginning of seeing his dream of one day becoming an artist turning into a reality.

Just before they went into their homeroom, Curtis stopped suddenly. Melanie could tell he had something to say. When he cleared his throat three times, she also suspected what he was about to say wasn't easy. At first, he held his head down, but then he slowly lifted it so that he could see Melanie face-to-face.

"Thanks for helping on the poster. You did a good . . . I mean, a great job."

Though she was not known for holding her tongue, Melanie suddenly found herself speechless. There were only three words she managed to let escape from her mouth.

"Thank you, Curtis," she said softly.

In that one brief moment, Melanie had seen another side of Curtis Givens. He wasn't mean or nasty or rude. In fact, he wasn't any of the words that the other kids often used to describe him. And she was sorry for the times she had used those very words when talking about him to Kevin.

At this special moment in time, Curtis Givens was acting like a friend. And that made Melanie happy. *Maybe*, Melanie thought, *Kevin had been right all along.* She also thought about something Mrs. Blake would sometimes say. She couldn't remember all of the words, but she knew it had something to do with taking the time to read an entire book before saying it was no good.

Melanie realized there was more to Curtis Givens than what she had seen with her eyes. She had not taken the time to read his whole story. That made her promise she would never be so judgmental again. So as the two of them went inside the class and took their seats, they waited with bated breath for what could be the biggest announcement of their lives.

Chapter 13

AND THE WINNER IS . . .

BREAKFAST WAS FINALLY OVER. And now Kevin understood why Melanie and Curtis had decided to skip going into the cafeteria that morning. He couldn't eat a thing. And when he tried to drink his milk, he couldn't even swallow it. Kevin was just too nervous about waiting for the results of the contest. He gazed over at Jordan who had managed to finish his whole bowl of cereal. And he didn't look as if he had a nervous bone in his body. For the first time ever, Kevin would have been willing to trade places with his little brother.

Soon Mrs. Blake arrived to pick up her class. She took Jordan's hand, and with a little coaxing, the rest of the children put themselves in single file and prepared to follow her down the hall and into the classroom. Before she left the cafeteria, Mrs. Blake gave Kevin a "thumbs-up." It was her way of sending best wishes and support for the group's entry in the contest.

"Thanks, Mrs. Blake," he shouted as he raced off to class. Getting that extra encouragement from Mrs. Blake made Kevin feel like he was on top of the world.

Once everyone in the school was seated in their homeroom classes, it was time for the morning announcements. The direction was given to stand for the Pledge of Allegiance. As always, after its completion, there would be further school-related news. There was no mistaking how anxious Curtis was. He signaled for everyone to be quiet right after they finished saying the pledge.

"This is it!" he said, rubbing his hands together. "They're gonna tell us who won the contest!"

He looked over at Melanie and she looked back. Their thoughts were filled with scenes depicting the moment they would be awarded their prizes. Curtis visualized himself standing before the whole student body with his hands outstretched as he waited for the judges to place the prizewinning check and ribbon in his care. *What if someone asks me to give a speech?* he thought. *What would I say?*

Surely if ever there was an occasion calling for some awesome words from an accomplished artist, winning this contest would be it. He smiled when he remembered that Melanie was the talker in the group. So what would be better than allowing her to give the acceptance speech on behalf of all of them? Curtis was having a daydream and it was a pleasing one.

Meanwhile, Melanie was immersed in a daydream of her own. She saw herself accepting the prize money and the ribbon for the group. But more than that, she was glad to hear the photographer say when the picture appeared in the newspaper that it would be printed in color because a black-and-white photo couldn't do justice to the beautiful colors in her Kente outfit. He told her the colors were so exquisite, everyone should see them.

Hearing Principal Tate clearing his voice brought Melanie and Curtis back to the present. They knew it was time for that all-important moment to finally happen. Neither of them had to wonder if Kevin was listening; they knew he was "all ears."

Curtis took it upon himself to announce, "Principal Tate's gonna tell the names of the winners for the contest." He crossed the first two fingers on each of his hands and closed his eyes. One could easily tell that Curtis was making a wish, and it was probably the biggest wish he'd ever made in his entire life. Over on the other side of the room, Melanie slightly bowed her head and said a prayer that their entry would be the big winner.

When Principal Tate began to speak, there was complete silence in the room. "Boys and girls, we are so proud of the seriousness you've shown in entering the district-wide art contest. Because of the excellent entries received, we have decided to hold an assembly this afternoon. At that time the grand prizewinner will be announced."

"What? They can't do that! We want to hear who won now!" Curtis exclaimed. In that one short announcement, Curtis and Melanie found themselves having to put their dream of accepting their prize on hold a little while longer. "We don't need no assembly," Curtis complained under his breath. "Just say who the winners are and give us our prize."

As difficult as it was, Curtis, Kevin, and Melanie would have to go through the entire morning and part of the afternoon before they would learn the final outcome of the contest. Curtis had figured, if the announcement was made early, he'd be able to get his class work done. Now he found himself unable to focus his thoughts on anything except finding out when they would finally be able to accept their prize.

Waiting to attend the assembly to find out the names of the winners pretty much ensured that none of Curtis's class work would get done. Kevin likened the wait to the last day of every school year when students and teachers alike listened for that final bell that signaled the start of summer vacation.

Getting through the day was hard for Melanie too but when 2:30 p.m. came around at last, the special assembly was finally going to begin. Students were to told to bring their book bags, sweaters, and jackets with them so they could be dismissed directly after the program. Each class was assigned a special place to sit in the auditorium.

From where Kevin sat, he could see Melanie and Curtis, but at first he couldn't see Jordan. Once he realized the kindergarten classes were seated on the floor in the very front, he felt relieved knowing his little brother was there. But the pangs of guilt that nagged him about removing Jordan's name from the poster wouldn't let go. In his heart Kevin knew this amazing moment rightfully belonged to Jordan too.

While teachers hustled to get everyone settled down and quiet, Curtis's eyes met with those of another student. This boy, who gave the impression he was a picture of calm, also sat with both palms perspiring from nervousness. It was obvious that he very much wanted to win the contest too. It was Alex Martinez and Curtis felt very uncomfortable having to sit so close to him.

After having survived the long delay to find out the results, the last thing he wanted was to have Alex staring at him minutes before the announcement. But after giving it a little more thought, Curtis realized maybe having Alex next to him wasn't so bad. At least this way, when the judges called his name, Alex would at last get his just desert for all the times he had ridiculed and made fun of Curtis.

Seated in the very front of the auditorium was a panel of four judges. There were two women and two men. Kevin even recognized one of them as Mayor Perrine, whose picture he had seen many times in the local newspaper. Directly behind the judges' table were the four posters chosen as the contest finals. And although not surprised, Kevin, Curtis, and Melanie were certainly pleased to see their entry proudly displayed among the other finalists.

Curtis sat feeling confident knowing his dream was about to come true. He watched intently as one of the judges picked up the poster that his group created and held it alongside one of the others. At that moment, he had no idea if this action by the committee meant their group's picture was in the running for first or whether it had already been relegated to last place.

Soon, however, the mystery was over. To the oohs and aahs of the audience, everyone witnessed one of the judges place third and fourth place ribbons on the other two posters. It was apparent, the two they now passed among themselves were the first and second place winners.

Suddenly, winning for Curtis became even more critical. The other poster that the judges held in their hands was the entry submitted by none other than Alex Martinez. Curtis wondered why it had to come down to *that poster* drawn by *that student*. If he lost to anyone else, he knew he could handle it. But Alex Martinez was another story. If Alex was declared the winner, he'd have to listen to his bragging for weeks or maybe even months to come.

Curtis was convinced that if his group won, their winning would extend far beyond a ribbon and the prize money. For once, he would have beaten Alex at something and he'd have something that proved he was a winner. Never again would anyone be able to call Curtis Givens a loser.

All of the judges shook their heads and Curtis could tell they'd come to a decision. When one of the judges stood up, he knew the grand announcement he'd been waiting to hear all day was about to fall from the tongue of the serious looking man now positioned before the entire staff and student body of Harriet Tubman Elementary School.

Then the man spoke. "On behalf of the judging committee for the great city of Philadelphia, it is my pleasure to announce the winner of this year's 'Kids Helping Kids' poster contest." With both hands, he proudly held up the poster that had been unanimously selected.

"We won!" Curtis yelled, jumping out of his seat. "We won!" He stepped out into the aisle and headed to the front of the auditorium. He was immediately joined by Melanie and Kevin. Then Curtis did something that no one could have predicted. He walked over to where Jordan was sitting and offered his hand to help him up. Willingly, Jordan allowed Curtis to lead him up front with the others so he could take his rightful place.

Mayor Perrine shook hands with each of them. "Let me congratulate you on a job well done!" he said enthusiastically.

Kevin turned slightly to his left and saw the three remaining judges suddenly looking very somber. Their faces were stoic and covered in concern. This new development caused Kevin to suddenly get a very bad feeling in the pit of his stomach. It was different from the nervousness he'd felt earlier. This time, he actually felt sick. He could tell something was wrong and knew his suspicions were correct when one of the lady judges came and whispered something in the mayor's ear. He was sure it meant trouble.

First, he slightly bowed his head, touched Kevin on the shoulder and said, "I'm sorry, young man." He then stepped before the microphone to make an announcement. "There has been a correction. The first place prize will be awarded to entry number sixty-two. Unfortunately, the rules of the contest stipulated that participants were to be in grades four through six. And while we admire the creativity and applaud the wonderful entry submitted by this group, we have no other choice but to disqualify it. Would Mr. Alexander Martinez, the contestant who submitted poster number sixty-two, please come forth?"

It was devastating for Kevin to think their group had won— then only seconds later to learn that they'd been disqualified. This was more than he could take. It was like having tons of salt poured into a fresh wound. And when he saw Alex Martinez coming forth to claim the first place prize, he knew firsthand how bad Curtis was feeling too. Nothing could have made losing feel worse.

Wearing an enormous grin, Alex came to the front of the auditorium to accept the prize money and his first place ribbon. Curtis didn't even want to look at him; he had memorized that awful expression Alex wore every time he beat him at something. And, unfortunately, that was all the time.

"But you said we won," Melanie spoke up.

"And you would have," the mayor said almost in a whisper while calmly waving them to their seats. "But the judges realized when you all came up to claim your prize, the little fellow in your group didn't meet the grade level requirement as it was stated in the rules."

"But Jordan worked as hard as we did," Kevin told him.

The judges looked at the four children with regret. The mayor glanced again at their poster and at Alex's entry. One of the other judges came and stood beside him. He knew there was nothing he could do or say to change the rules.

"I'm sorry children," the judge said. "I . . . we, have no choice but to disqualify your entry. Once again, I am so very sorry."

Curtis heard the word "disqualify" and, although he was only kind of sure what it meant, he knew with absolute certainty —by the sound of the word—they had lost. Without saying anything else, he quietly returned to his seat and watched the judge place the satiny bright blue ribbon on Alex's poster and hand him a check for $150. With deep sadness, Kevin led Jordan back to where his class was sitting, while Melanie followed and took her seat.

The day they had dreamed about and worked so hard for had come crashing down all around them in just a matter of minutes. Once again, Curtis thought about losing to Alex and it made him feel sick on the inside. Melanie took her seat next to him and hung her head. Curtis pressed his hands firmly against the sides of his face and closed his eyes. He tried to hide how bad he was feeling, but Melanie could see that he was crying.

She leaned over and whispered in his ear. "I don't care what nobody says, we still had the best poster." Hearing that made

Curtis feel a little better, but way down deep on the inside, he believed it might take him the rest of his life to get over what had just happened. Never before had he been so close to being declared a winner. And for Curtis Givens, the taste of victory, although only for a few brief moments, had allowed him to know what it felt like to be on top of the world.

Chapter 14

COMING ACROSS JORDAN

MRS. BLAKE WAS PLEASED to see that in spite of the tremendous disappointment the children had suffered in losing the art contest, they still came by her room in the afternoon to draw and color to the accompaniment of classical selections from Mozart.

Close to three weeks had passed and she found herself feeling especially proud of Curtis. He had managed to stay out of detention and hadn't been assigned to the "time-out" table during lunch period anymore. He now sat with Melanie and Kevin. One thing, however, remained the same. Alex Martinez somehow always managed to find time to linger his way past their table and dig in his heels with one of his negative comments. It was his way of reminding Curtis what he thought of him.

Alex was pretty clever because he didn't always speak out loud. Sometimes he'd just walk by wearing that sly grin that made Curtis want to cringe. His expression all by itself said plenty.

Fortunately, Mrs. Blake's promise of all the drawing paper he could hold was enough to keep Curtis at peace and strengthen him with enough power to ignore Alex. Mrs. Blake said if he worked hard in his classes and earned good grades, he was welcome to come after school to draw any time he wanted. And Curtis made sure he was at her door ready to draw every day.

Both Mrs. Blake and Principal Tate were happy that Curtis was doing so well at keeping his part of the bargain. The reports coming from his teachers were good. And one look at his grades revealed he was serious about his studies. Thankfully, it hadn't been a difficult choice for him to make. By now he really liked going to Mrs. Blake's room, probably as much as Melanie did.

Thanks to Mrs. Blake, Curtis and Kevin got a chance to sketch all kinds of drawings and letters in the block and bubble styles they liked to create. She would often hang up their artwork on the bulletin board in back of her desk. When she did, she would sometimes catch Jordan smiling as he recognized some of the coloring he'd done. On one occasion, he slowly walked past her desk, softly brushed his small hand across one of the pictures, and said, "me."

Curtis must have been trying to heal the hurt he felt from losing the contest because he didn't even mention it anymore. But no matter how well he managed to cover his feelings, Melanie and Kevin could tell he was still in a whole lot of pain. In fact, though she didn't ask, Melanie often wondered why Curtis had brought Jordan up front during the assembly for everyone to see when it had been his idea to take Jordan's name off the poster in the first place. No one would have ever known and they wouldn't have been disqualified. Even when Mrs. Blake apologized for missing the grade requirement, Curtis was the first one in the group to admit they had known about it. He also confessed that it was his idea to remove Jordan's name from the poster. The only thing that seemed to make Curtis feel better was drawing. When he drew, he did so quietly; careful to put all of his concentration into the pictures he created.

Kevin would follow his lead and add scenery to Curtis's intricate drawings of people. Once the scene was done, Melanie and Jordan would color with such exactness, it was almost impossible to detect even the slightest evidence of coloring outside the lines. Once they were finished, the four of them would take their picture and present it to Mrs. Blake, who in turn, would make a big fuss and remind them of what wonderful talented artists they were.

On this particular afternoon while Melanie and Jordan fed the fish, Curtis and Kevin were busy sketching something new. They were all so involved in their activities that none of the children noticed the well-dressed gentleman speaking with Mrs. Blake at her desk. If Melanie hadn't run out of fish food on the third shake of the container, she would have never become curious.

"I'll be right back, Jordan," she said, hurrying to the front of the room. Not wanting to interrupt, she stood quietly, just a few feet away from Mrs. Blake and her interesting guest. Suddenly, Mrs. Blake stopped her conversation and pointed.

"Mr. Chaney, this is Melanie. She is one of the four students who worked on the poster. Would you like to meet the others?"

"I would very much like to meet them, thank you."

Before Mrs. Blake got the chance to tell Melanie to ask the others to come to her desk, Melanie had already gone to the back of the room to get the boys. She must have sensed something good was about to happen because by the time she reached them, she was bursting at the seams with excitement and spilling over with happiness.

"Mrs. Blake wants to see you two."

Kevin immediately stopped and hurried to get Jordan. "C'mon, Jordan," he said. "Mrs. Blake wants to talk to us."

Melanie noticed that Curtis didn't move. "She wants to see you too, Curtis."

"What for?" he asked.

"I don't know but she said for all of us to come."

Curtis made a face that said he just wanted to be left alone to draw. He put his pencil down and reluctantly got up off the floor.

"Okay," he said, "I'm comin'."

When Curtis reached Mrs. Blake's desk, he was met with a warm greeting from the well-dressed man.

"So," he said confidently, "this young man must be Curtis." He reached out to shake Curtis's hand. "Nice to meet you, Curtis."

Curtis didn't know what to make of the formal greeting, but nevertheless he shook the man's hand firmly.

"Hello," he answered softly.

Mrs. Blake was wearing a huge smile and holding something in her hand. "This is Mr. Miles Chaney. He's from the Cultural Arts and Center City Beautification Committee." The children stared at her curiously, wondering what such a long title had to do with any of them. "He was also one of the judges for the Philadelphia school district-wide poster contest you entered.

Maybe you remember him."

As soon as Mrs. Blake mentioned the poster contest, Curtis got that terrible feeling in his stomach again. He didn't want to hear anything else about it.

"I thought I seen him somewhere before," he growled. "I'm goin' back to draw." Curtis wondered how things were ever going to get back to normal if every time he tried to forget, somebody brought up the contest again. More than anything he just wanted to go back to his drawing and be left alone. But the minute Curtis got ready to turn around and leave his eyes met Mrs. Blake's. So instead of walking away, he apologized for being rude.

"Sorry, Mister."

"Mr. Chaney stopped by to return your poster," Mrs. Blake said proudly, handing it to Melanie. From the moment she noticed Jordan's name written on back, her eyes made contact with Curtis's eyes. When he dropped his head, Melanie was sure he had gone back to Mr. Snead's office and added Jordan's name.

Melanie moved closer to Jordan. "Thank you," she said politely.

"No," Mr. Chaney interrupted, "Thank you."

". . . for what?" Kevin asked.

Mr. Chaney looked over at Mrs. Blake and smiled. "Thank you for allowing the people of Philadelphia to enjoy your extraordinary artwork."

"But we lost," Curtis blurted out. "We didn't win."

Mr. Chaney bent down slightly and placed his hand on Curtis's shoulder. "Sometimes, young man, what we see as a defeat is really a victory waiting to be turned inside out."

The children wondered what Mr. Chaney meant by the peculiar words he spoke. How could their loss, especially a loss to Alex Martinez, be seen as any kind of victory?

"I've spoken to Mr. Tate and to Mrs. Blake. Letters were sent to your parents requesting permission to allow your school to take a special field trip. That trip will take place tomorrow morning and I hope you'll all want to go."

"A trip to where?" Kevin asked.

"That part," said a smiling Mr. Chaney, "will have to wait until tomorrow. It's a surprise."

"Please tell us, Mrs. Blake," Melanie begged. "We don't wanna wait till tomorrow."

"I'm afraid you'll have to," she said. "My lips are sealed. I *can* tell you, though, that in the morning, there will be busses for each of your homerooms waiting to take us on the field trip."

Though she didn't have a clue where they would be going, Melanie began clapping her hands happily just because she loved going on field trips.

"I can hardly wait!" she declared.

"I guess it'll be fun," Kevin said optimistically. "Won't it, Jordan?"

Mr. Chaney was ready to leave. "So then, I'll see all of you bright and early tomorrow morning?"

"I know I'll be there!" Melanie said confidently.

Kevin was quick to agree. "And we'll be there too. Right, Jordan?"

Everyone was waiting for an answer from Curtis. He filled his cheeks with air and let out his answer. "Yeah, okay."

Mrs. Blake walked Mr. Chaney to the door. "Yes, Mr.

Chaney," she assured him. "We'll be there. And, thank you again."

Curtis didn't know what to think about what had just happened. He only knew he was probably going to have another tough night trying to go to sleep because he'd have to wait until morning to find out where they were going. *At least this time*, he thought, *I don't have to worry about losing another contest*. That was already done and over with.

As soon as Mr. Chaney left, Curtis returned to his drawing. He didn't show any interest in hearing anything else about the mysterious field trip.

Mrs. Blake told the others they could return to their activities and did something she knew would make Curtis feel better. She put on some classical music and allowed Curtis the peace to do what he loved doing more than anything else in the world—she let him draw.

When the children arrived at school the next morning, the busses were waiting just as Mrs. Blake had told them they would be. Each one was carefully lining up directly in front of the school building. And many of the students thought it funny to see Mr. Tate acting like a traffic cop as he stood outside directing all the busses to their parking spaces to make sure they all fit.

Curtis, Kevin, and Melanie still hadn't figured out what was going on. But from the very second they entered the building, they could sense that something special was in the air. They could feel it all around them. Principal Tate had given special permission for the three of them to travel with Mrs. Blake's class. This way, they could ride together with Jordan.

Curtis was especially glad that he wouldn't have to ride on the same bus as Alex. As good as he was feeling on this day, he didn't want to give Alex even the tiniest chance of spoiling it. Since the contest had ended, he'd done everything he could to stay out of his path. And Curtis was determined to keep it that way.

He was really glad about riding with his friends. *At least*, he told himself, *I won't have to listen to Alex telling me what a great artist he is.* And the worst part of hearing Alex brag was knowing he had a blue ribbon and prize money to prove it.

As the students filed into the cafeteria, Curtis and Melanie were glad there was nothing to feel nervous about. So there was no reason to skip breakfast on this day. Kevin walked Jordan over to his group and then joined Melanie and Curtis at their table.

Mrs. Brundidge came out of the kitchen carrying a tray of warm blueberry muffins. She went directly to the table where Melanie, Kevin, and Curtis sat. "Here, we are. Deez es for you for a day so very special."

"Thank you, Mrs. B," they all said.

Kevin nudged Melanie. "Why'd Mrs. Brundidge make us muffins?"

"I dunno, but it sure was nice of her."

She looked over at Curtis who had already pretty much finished his. "That was real nice of Mrs. Brundidge wasn't it, Curtis?"

"Yeah," he said with his mouth still full and blueberries on his front teeth. "Real nice!"

"What you did for Jordan was real nice too."

"Thanks, Curtis," said Kevin. "Thanks for including Jordan.

I know how much you wanted to win the contest."

Curtis shook his head yes letting Melanie and Kevin know he was okay and ate what was left of his muffin.

Melanie looked at Kevin and Curtis with an expression that went beyond curious. "I wonder, what's going on?"

"Whattaya mean?" Kevin asked, finishing his muffin.

"Everybody knows Mrs. Brundidge only bakes when something real special is going on. Like when the governor visited our school last year."

"Melanie's right," Curtis blurted out. "And why'd she only give muffins to us?"

"I know why," said Kevin. "She probably still feels sorry about us losing the contest."

Melanie tried to keep the boys feeling positive. "Whatever her reason was, it was real nice of her anyway."

Kevin and Curtis shook their heads yes and picked at the few little crumbs left in the muffin papers they held in their hands. When they saw Mrs. Blake enter the cafeteria, they knew the bell signaling the start of homeroom was about to ring. The three of them gathered up their papers and juice containers and threw them in the trash can.

On their way out of the cafeteria, they stopped to speak to Mrs. Blake, while hoping to get some answers to their questions. But before they reached her, Mrs. Brundidge once again came hurrying out of the kitchen.

"You liked de muffins, yes?" There was a special gleam in her eyes that let the children know how important their response was to her.

"They were great!" Melanie said, rubbing her stomach.

"Can ya make some more tomorrow?" Curtis asked.

"Yeah, please?" Kevin echoed.

Mrs. Brundidge grinned the way she always did when she knew the children enjoyed her special treats. "Dis was for dis special day. It vas my gift to you all."

Obviously left in the dark by Mrs. Brundidge's comment, they thanked her again and hurried to catch up with Mrs. Blake. They could see her class was about to leave.

"Good morning, Mrs. Blake," Kevin called.

"Hi, Mrs. Blake," Melanie cheered.

Curtis simply put up his hand as a gesture to say hello.

Mrs. Blake continued leading her class out of the cafeteria. "Are you all excited about the field trip this morning?"

"Me and Kevin are," Melanie told her. "And Jordan is too! But I dunno about Curtis. He might be. He won't say. Can you tell us now where we're going?"

"If I did that, it wouldn't be much of a surprise, now would it?"

Melanie was starting to feel like something really wonderful was about to happen. And she tried to lift Curtis's spirits. "Did you hear that, Curtis? Mrs. Blake said she didn't want to mess up the surprise. It's something really good. I just know it!"

"Yeah . . . sure," Curtis said softly. He really wanted to believe for something good like Melanie did. When he glanced over at Kevin, he saw that he was sporting a big smile too.

Whatever the two of them were thinking, it was pretty obvious they were starting to believe the four of them were somehow connected to the special surprise. Kevin patted his little brother gently on his shoulder. "Hope you're ready, Jordan."

Mrs. Blake knew it was almost time for them to leave. "I

want you three to report to your homeroom classes," she said. "After attendance is taken, your teachers will allow you to report to my room and we will board the bus."

Mrs. Blake didn't have to say another word. Kevin, Curtis, and Melanie headed straight to homeroom. They were eager to get on the bus and find out where it was going to take them.

As soon as they were dismissed, the three of them went directly to Mrs. Blake's room and lined up with her students. "Mrs. Blake, is it okay if I sit with Jordan?" Kevin asked.

"Yes, Kevin, you may sit with your brother."

"What about us?" Curtis asked, giving the impression that he didn't want to feel left out. "I thought we was gonna sit together."

Melanie quickly offered a solution. "We can sit on the seat in the back. We can all fit!"

Everyone agreed and the minute they got on the bus, they immediately headed for the back to claim the big, long seat.

"I wanna sit by the window," Melanie demanded. "And I called it first."

Kevin didn't seem too happy.

"What's da matter with you?" Curtis asked. "I ain't taken up for a girl, but she *did* call it first."

"Jordan likes lookin' out the window when we ride places. He don't say nothing, but I can see that he likes lookin' at all the stuff out there."

Melanie stood up and moved aside. "Here ya go, Jordan. You can have the window." Then she pointed at the space next to him. "And Kevin, you can sit right there."

"Thanks," he said, putting his arm around his little brother.

Melanie moved aside so that Curtis could sit next to Kevin. "That's okay," he said, refusing the third space on the seat. "You sit there."

"Thank you, Curtis," said Melanie.

"It's okay."

When the bus driver started the motor, the squeals of laughter from the children coupled with all the excitement was almost deafening. Next, the wheels began turning, indicating the journey had begun. Leaving the front of Harriet Tubman Elementary School were eight busloads of teachers, students, parents, and Mr. Tate.

But it was the first bus in line that held Kevin, Curtis, Melanie, and Jordan. Their eyes widened in anticipation of what was in store. As the bus passed by familiar scenes around the city of Philadelphia, Curtis and Kevin pointed and named some of the places they knew.

Melanie, not wanting to be outdone, also joined in. "Look! Over there," she shouted. "That's the Philadelphia Doll Museum. I've been there; they've got all kinds of dolls!"

Neither Curtis nor Kevin gave any attention to Melanie's announcement. However, a few minutes later, she soon made another and both boys were all ears. "And that place over there is called, 'The Arts Garage.' I ain't never been there, but I bet there's a whole lotta art stuff in there."

"Wow!" they said at the same time.

After traveling for what seemed like about twenty-five minutes, the wheels of the busses came to a sudden halt. First, Jordan tapped both hands on the window and pressed his face against the glass.

"Me! Me!" he shouted. "You!" he shouted again.

Kevin stood up in amazement and so did Curtis and Melanie.

"I don't believe it!" Curtis yelled. He tried to get closer to the window as the driver parked the bus. He pressed his face hard against the glass.

"Look!" he shouted. "It's our picture!"

Kevin placed his hand gently on Jordan's shoulder, leaned down, and whispered in his brother's ear. "It's you, little brother. It's me. It's all of us."

Mrs. Blake led the children carefully off the bus and allowed Melanie, Curtis, Kevin, and Jordan to stand in front the enormous building on whose side bared an exact replica of the children's poster. Nothing but oohs and aahs could be heard as the remaining busses unloaded to let everyone get a look at the gigantic mural that adorned the side of the building.

Every color and every part of the original poster had been copied for the entire city to see. There before everyone was Curtis reaching out his hand to help Melanie, who was reaching out her hand to help Kevin, who was reaching out his hand to help Jordan, who was reaching out his hand to help another child climb a mountain.

Kevin saw his brother smiling and knew Jordan understood they had done something good. And they had done it together.

Curtis took his hands and tried to wipe his eyes without anyone seeing him. He walked over to where Mrs. Blake was standing and touched her hand.

"Thank you for the prayers, Mrs. Blake. You were right about God sometimes givin' us something better." With the entire student body from Harriet Tubman Elementary School watching, he stared up at the building and declared, "I don't think nothin' coulda topped this."

Mrs. Blake shook her head in agreement. "You mean the mural?"

"No," Curtis said, pointing at little Jordan who was jumping up and down joyfully. "The happiness that's comin' outta Jordan."

Mr. Tate called for Kevin, Melanie, Curtis, and Jordan to come forth. And when they did, the mayor of the great city of Philadelphia awarded each one of them a certificate, pinned on each of them a shiny, blue satiny ribbon, and handed them $150 each.

As they posed for the newspaper photographers, Curtis looked out at the crowd and saw Alex Martinez. The smirk was gone and Curtis knew there was nothing Alex could ever say again to make him feel like less than the great artist he knew that he was. Melanie stood proudly beside him adorned in her colorful Kente, knowing she had come across her greatest discovery yet—the wonderful friends she'd found in Kevin, Curtis, and of course—little Jordan.

Kevin had positioned himself where he could see every detail; he simply stood and stared up at the amazing mural. Tenderly, he put his arm around Jordan. "That's us," he said. "That's us."

In the midst of the applause and the cheering coming from the onlookers, the two brothers were silent. Suddenly, Kevin felt Jordan's small arm reach around his, and he knew his little brother was happy and proud of their accomplishment.

Kevin smiled, knowing God had opened a very special door and allowed them to experience a joy that some might say was impossible.

RUN, JEREMIAH RUN!

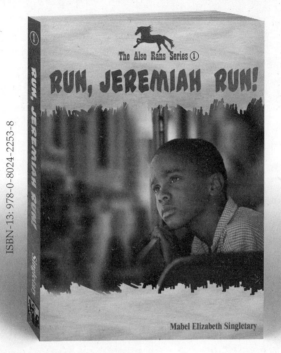

As a foster child, life for Jeremiah is a garbage bag filled with his things, a new school, and worst of all finding a new family. Jeremiah holds on to his grandmother's promise of a handful of mustard seeds being planted one day to grow into a tree of his own. After being expelled from school again, he thinks that no one will want him to be a part of their family. With the help of his friends, he learns about teamwork and what it means to persevere.

WWW.LIFTEVERYVOICEBOOKS.COM

1-800-678-8812 · MOODYPUBLISHERS.COM

JUST JUMP

ISBN-13: 978-0-8024-2251-4

The girls of the Double Dutch Club are going to compete in the state competition! What begins as a desire to win a coveted trophy becomes the foundation for relationships that last a lifetime.

SOMETHING TO JUMP ABOUT

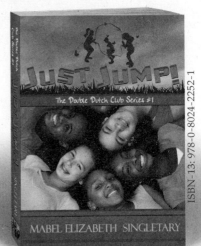

ISBN-13: 978-0-8024-2252-1

The girls from Just Jump return to school and learn that Ming, their wise leader, has moved away. They'll need a new girl to jump Double Dutch with them in time for the December Jump Off.

WWW.LIFTEVERYVOICEBOOKS.COM

1-800-678-8812 · MOODYPUBLISHERS.COM

A PROMISE AND A RAINBOW

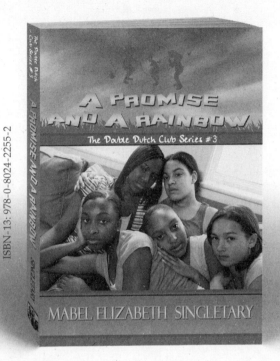

INTRODUCING THE NEWEST RELEASE IN THE DOUBLE DUTCH CLUB SERIES!
The Double Dutch Club is saddened by the thought of Rachel having to leave
for the summer. And Rachel is trying to remain excited about
the Double Dutch Club winning the North Carolina "Jump Off."

WWW.LIFTEVERYVOICEBOOKS.COM
1-800-678-8812 · MOODYPUBLISHERS.COM

The Negro National Anthem

Lift every voice and sing
Till earth and heaven ring,
Ring with the harmonies of Liberty;
Let our rejoicing rise
High as the listening skies,
Let it resound loud as the rolling sea.
Sing a song full of the faith that the dark past has taught us,
Sing a song full of the hope that the present has brought us,
Facing the rising sun of our new day begun
Let us march on till victory is won.

So begins the Black National Anthem, by James Weldon Johnson in 1900. Lift Every Voice is the name of the joint imprint of The Institute for Black Family Development and Moody Publishers.

Our vision is to advance the cause of Christ through publishing African-American Christians who educate, edify, and disciple Christians in the church community through quality books written for African Americans.

Since 1988, the Institute for Black Family Development, a 501(c)(3) non-profit Christian organization, has been providing training and technical assistance for churches and Christian organizations. The Institute for Black Family Development's goal is to become a premier trainer in leadership development, management, and strategic planning for pastors, ministers, volunteers, executives, and key staff members of churches and Christian organizations. To learn more about The Institute for Black Family Development, write us at:

The Institute for Black Family Development
15151 Faust
Detroit, Michigan 48223

We hope you enjoy this book from Moody Publishers. Our goal is to provide high-quality, thought-provoking books and products that connect truth to your real needs and challenges. For more information on other books and products written and produced from a biblical perspective, go to www.moodypublishers.com or write to:

Moody Publishers/LEV
820 N. LaSalle Boulevard
Chicago, IL 60610
www.moodypublishers.com